PENNINGTON

A CHARMING COUNTRY TOWN – BUT WHAT SECRETS LIE BENEATH?

Imagine...

A picturesque spa town and pretty villages that nestle deep in the heart of England.

Pennington Country...

In Pennington the streets are filled with old-fashioned buildings, attractive tearooms and irresistible shops. In the surrounding villages of Chastlecombe, Stavely and Swancote elegant manor houses rub shoulders with cosy stone cottages, and all the gardens are ablaze with flowers.

Pennington Lives...

And beneath the smooth surface the passions run high – overwhelming attraction, jealousy, desire, anger...and once-in-a-lifetime love.

Next month in Catherine George's
Pennington series:
BARGAINING WITH THE BOSS

Catherine George was born in Wales, and early on developed a passion for reading which eventually fuelled her compulsion to write. Marriage to an engineer led to nine years in Brazil, but on his later travels the education of her son and daughter kept her in the UK. And instead of constant reading to pass her lonely evenings she began to write the first of her romantic novels. When not writing and reading she loves to cook, listen to opera, browse in antique shops and walk the Labrador.

She has written over 60 romantic novels.

Praise for Catherine George:

'Catherine George...keeps readers thoroughly entranced.'
—*Romantic Times*

'Ms George has a captivating way of leaving her readers wanting more.'
—*www.theromancereadersconnection.com*

The Forever Affair

by
Catherine George

MILLS & BOON®

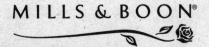

MILLS & BOON and MILLS & BOON with the Rose Device are registered trademarks of the publisher.

First published in Great Britain 1998. This edition 2003.
Harlequin Mills & Boon Limited,
Eton House, 18-24 Paradise Road, Richmond, Surrey, TW9 1SR

© Catherine George 1998

ISBN 0 263 83695 9

144-0304

Printed and bound in Spain
by Litografia Rosés S.A., Barcelona

Dear Reader

Following (humbly) the example of Thomas Hardy and his Casterbridge, I decided to create my own fictional town for the location of many of my novels. The result is the Cotswolds town of Pennington Spa, a place of thriving modern commerce located in classical buildings which, like its Pump Rooms, date from the Regency era, when drinking the waters was all the rage. Having lived in two attractive county towns in the past, I've taken features from both and added fictional ones of my own to invent a town of wide streets, leafy squares and crescents, with buildings in the local golden stone and public gardens bright with seasonal flowers. There are several hotels, numerous restaurants, parks, cinemas, a theatre and, of course, irresistible specialist shops which sell clothes, jewellery, contemporary furniture and fine art, alongside others which offer bargains to the antiques hunter.

To me, Pennington and its nearby towns and villages – Chastlecombe, Swancote, Stavely, Abbots Munden – are the dream combination of prosperity and timeless charm. I just wish Pennington really existed, so I could live there.

Best wishes

Catherine George

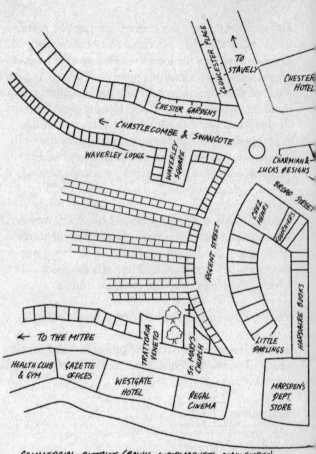

TO
STAVELY

GLOUCESTER PLACE

CHESTER
HOTEL

CHESTER GARDENS

← CHASTLECOMBE & SWANCOTE

WAVERLEY LODGE

WAVERLEY SQUARE

CHARMIAN &
LUCAS DESIGNS

BROAD STREET

CHEZ HENRI

FOURNIER'S

REGENT STREET

HARDACRE BOOKS

LITTLE
DARLINGS

← TO THE MITRE

TRATTORIA VENETO

ST MARY'S CHURCH

HEALTH CLUB
& GYM

GAZETTE
OFFICES

WESTGATE
HOTEL

REGAL
CINEMA

MARSDEN'S
DEPT.
STORE

COMMERCIAL DISTRICT (BANKS, SUPERMARKETS, CHAIN STORES)

CHAPTER ONE

WATCHING television with her brother had not been part of Catrin's original plan for her Saturday night. At this hour she should have been at the party thrown by her boss and his wife to celebrate their silver wedding. And enjoying it with Julian, invited specifically as her escort. But by eleven, when it was obvious Julian wasn't going to turn up, Catrin made excuses, expressed thanks, left the party and took a taxi back to Liam, who was staying with her, courtesy of a flu epidemic at his school.

Her friend Dinah, who had gladly volunteered to keep young Liam company for the evening, was ensconced alongside him on the sofa, and apparently as engrossed in the soccer match as the boy. But something in Dinah's posture made it clear she was determined to sit it out until Liam was in bed and she could demand explanations.

At last the programme was over, and a reluctant Liam sent off to Catrin's room.

'So talk,' commanded Dinah when they were alone. 'You can't settle down for the night until I get off your sofabed, so what happened?'

'Julian didn't show,' said Catrin bitterly. 'After all the money I wasted on fine feathers, too.'

'At least the shoes were in the sale,' consoled Dinah.

'They still cost a fortune!' Catrin's smile was crooked. 'And I splurged on the dress because someone once told me my eyes match when I wear green.'

'He was right.'

'How do you know it was a he?'

'Educated guess!'

Dinah, who was handsome, forty-something and amicably divorced, eyed Catrin thoughtfully. 'So Julian didn't show. How, exactly, do you feel about him?'

'At the moment, annoyed!' Catrin paused, thinking it over. 'But I could be in love with him, I think, if I put my mind to it.'

'Then you're not,' Dinah assured her.

'Which is all to the good, in the circumstances.' Catrin frowned, then jumped up, sniffing suspiciously. 'Can you smell smoke?'

Dinah sniffed in turn, then shot to her feet. 'I can, indeed. And Liam's a bit young to be smoking in there.'

She ran into the bedroom to check on him while Catrin flew into the kitchen to do a spot check on her various appliances. All was in order, but to her alarm the smell of smoke was growing stronger by the minute. Catrin pulled up the window blind to look out and gasped in horror. Flames were shooting up from the flat below.

'*Dinah!* Get Liam out of here right now,' she

yelled. 'I'll ring for the fire brigade. The ground-floor flat's on fire.'

Dinah promptly yanked a protesting Liam out of bed, snatched up his slippers and dressing gown, and hurried him from the bedroom. She thrust the boy before her out onto the smoke-filled landing, soothing him as he called urgently to his sister to follow them.

'I'm coming!' shouted Catrin, a second before the kitchen window exploded inwards in a shower of flames and splintered glass. She dropped the phone with a scream and catapulted out of the flat, slamming the door behind her, horrified to find she couldn't see a thing through the dense smoke in the stairwell.

Coughing and choking, fighting to stay calm, she made her way blindly down the first flight of stairs, terrified a wall of flame would envelop her at any minute. Scorching heat came up to meet her, but thoughts of Liam and Dinah sent her careering down the remaining stairs after them, until her frivolous heels skidded on the smooth stone and she flailed wildly, gagging on smoke as she lost her balance and plummeted downwards, bumping helplessly into walls and balustrade as she went until her head came into sharp contact with something which knocked her out.

Catrin fought her way through a series of nightmares where someone kept pushing a mask back over her face, and asking her name. When she couldn't remember it voices told her not to worry, to keep perfectly still, then there was a pricking of needles and someone talking soothingly while her forehead was stitched, then the welcome darkness came back. When she woke up fully at last she was in a hospital bed screened by curtains, and it was bright daylight. Screened off, she thought, frowning. Was she dying? She coughed convulsively, and regretted it. Her chest burned, it hurt to heave in breath, and her head ached abominably, and *Liam*! Where was Liam?

A nurse popped her head through the curtains. 'Ah, you're awake.'

'My brother!' croaked Catrin urgently. 'Liam. Is he all right?'

'Your memory's come back! Splendid,' said the nurse, beaming. 'And don't worry about your brother. He's in the waiting room with Mrs Martin. He's fine. So's your friend. They can come and see you in a minute.'

'What happened?' asked Catrin, coughing painfully. 'The fire—'

'Don't talk for a moment. Here comes Sister. She'll want a word.' The cheerful nurse vanished through the curtains, to be replaced by a calm young woman with an air of ineluctable authority.

'Good morning, I'm Sister Lockwood. I gather you've recovered your memory? Tell me your full name, please.'

'Catrin Julia Hughes.'

'Splendid. How are you feeling?'

Catrin drew in an unsteady, difficult breath. 'A bit battered.'

Sister Lockwood nodded briskly. 'As well you

might. A doctor will be in to check on you shortly, so I'll leave explanations until later. In the meantime, let Nurse give you some water and make you comfortable. Then you can see your brother and Mrs Martin. But only for a moment or two.'

When Liam came in with Dinah he looked subdued, despite a brand-new tracksuit, and looked as though he'd been scrubbed from head to foot. He surprised his sister by kissing her.

'Gosh, I must be ill,' croaked Catrin. 'Kisses yet!'

To Liam's mortification tears welled in his eyes. 'I thought you were dead, Cat,' he choked.

'Nine lives, that's me,' she assured him, as Dinah kissed her carefully, then drew a chair up to the bed.

'My word, you gave us a fright. Young Liam, here, thought the worst when one of the firefighters carried you out.' Dinah shuddered.

'It was those stupid shoes,' rasped Catrin ruefully. 'Pride goes before a fall and so on. What happened to the Morrisons?'

'They were out,' reported Liam, sniffing manfully. 'Their VCR was on, recording a film. The firefighters think the wiring shorted.'

'Are they all right?' asked Catrin anxiously.

'Apart from the shock of arriving home to find their flat gutted, they're fine,' said Dinah dryly. 'They were just in time to see you carried out unconscious. Needless to say they're absolutely hysterical with remorse about you, as well as shattered over losing their flat.'

'Poor young things,' said Catrin, and eyed her apprehensively. 'Tell me the worst. How's *my* place?'

'Smelly, and covered with soot and so on,' said Dinah, 'but the fire brigade arrived in time to save it.'

'Those firefighters are fab!' said Liam, brightening. 'They had to break down your door—'

'Wonderful,' said Catrin faintly.

'Don't worry,' soothed Dinah, 'it's already been repaired. The windows, too. Once we knew you were all right I took Liam home to my place for a scrub and a sleep—and some food, of course—then we went shopping for the tracksuit before we came back to you.' She glanced up at the sound of movement outside. 'We're about to get thrown out. I gather you're going to be kept in for a bit for observation, Catrin. Don't worry about Liam. He can stay with me. Do you want to contact your parents?'

'No. Pity to spoil their holiday.' Catrin looked at her brother. 'Unless you do, Liam?'

'Nah,' he said scornfully. 'I'll be fine with Dinah. And I go back to school next week, anyway. If I tell Mum and Dad about the fire they'll be back on the next plane.'

'True.' By this time Catrin was feeling tired, and Dinah noted it and got up.

'Come on, my lad. We'll go home and have a bite to eat, and come back later.'

To Catrin's surprise Liam leaned over and gave her another kiss, then flushed, embarrassed, as a tall, dark man in an elegant suit came in, followed by Sister, and a trio of weary-looking young men in white coats, with the young nurse bringing up the rear.

'Dr Hope-Ellison,' said Sister, as though she were announcing royalty.

The consultant physician smiled courteously at Liam and Dinah. 'Sorry to throw you out. Come back at visiting time and I promise not to intrude.'

Liam thanked him shyly, waved at Catrin, then followed Dinah out, leaving the patient rigid with shock.

The consultant exchanged a few remarks with Sister, then came to the patient's side, smiling down at her.

'How are you feeling?'

Catrin, who had lain with eyes firmly closed after one look at him, opened them reluctantly, hoping in vain she'd been mistaken. 'Not very wonderful,' she croaked.

Dr Hope-Ellison stared down at her, arrested. For a moment the entire scene was like a waxwork tableau as consultant and patient gazed at each other in shocked recognition, oblivious of the deeply interested entourage. As the silence lengthened there were curious looks from the other men, and Sister Lockwood coughed meaningfully, recalling the consultant to the matter in hand.

He assumed a courteous, professional smile as he took Catrin's hand to check her pulse and glanced at her chart. 'Dr Hawkins, here, tells me that last night you were brought into Casualty suffering from smoke inhalation and a head wound, Miss Hughes, plus concussion from your fall as you were escaping.'

'The roof didn't fall on me, then,' she muttered, flippant in an effort to control the pulse racing under the touch of his fingers, which tightened involuntarily for an instant, accelerating her pulse-rate even more.

'Is that what you thought had happened?' he asked casually, his eyes fixed firmly on his watch.

'It's the nearest way to describe how I feel.' In more ways than one, thought Catrin despairingly, and began to cough. The sister moved swiftly to give her some water before surrendering the reluctant patient to the consultant's examination. The nurse propped Catrin up and the consultant moved his stethoscope over her back and listened intently, then the patient was allowed to lie down again, shaky and breathless, and prey to so many warring sensations she'd never felt worse in her life.

'You were given oxygen and some blood tests,' Dr Hope-Ellison informed her crisply. 'But I don't antic-ipate lasting damage. Have you any questions?'

Yes, thought Catrin. Your name for starters. Last time I saw you it was Ashe. Second question, why did you break my heart all those years ago? It's mended now, of course. But no thanks to you. 'When can I go home?' she croaked.

'Once we're satisfied that you've recovered from the concussion.' His smile curved his mouth but stopped short of the black-lashed blue eyes which had once haunted her dreams. 'Don't worry, Miss Hughes, Dr Hawkins will monitor your progress. We won't keep you a moment longer than necessary.' He paused, as though he was about to add something, then thought better of it, and with a courteous nod he departed, his entourage following in his wake.

Catrin lay motionless, feeling giddy and sick, her head banging like a drum and her world turned upside-down. At this time the day before she had been shopping with Liam and Dinah, and looking forward to a party. Since then she'd not only escaped from a fire, she had actually met up with Ashe again. Only now he was Dr Hope-Ellison, for heaven's sake, consultant physician at the General. And he'd changed a lot. But then, so had she. Sometimes, over the past ten years, she had wondered if they'd ever meet again. But never in her wildest dreams had she imagined circumstances like these.

Ten years before Ashe had been a very handsome young man, but now the good looks had hardened and matured; the dark hair was streaked with silver at the temples. And the slate-blue eyes were just as arresting, but they held a glacially self-confident expression very different from the haggard charm of old. And I, thought Catrin bitterly, look like something the cat dragged in.

By the time Liam and Dinah arrived later that evening Catrin, washed, combed and fed, was chatting hoarsely with the other patients in the small ward.

'Gosh, Cat, what a shiner! It's all sort of purple now,' said Liam, grinning, and began arranging a basket of grapes and a pile of magazines on her side-table.

'I know,' she said despondently, having confronted her face with horror during the freshening up process.

'Glorious Technicolor. Mother wouldn't recognise me.'

'It's a lot better than what might have happened,' said Dinah firmly. 'By the way, everything's functioning in your flat. There was a message on your phone from Julian Fellowes. He was delayed in Germany and left a number for you to ring.'

Catrin looked at the scrap of paper without interest. Julian and the party seemed oddly distant, like something belonging to another life. Life before the fire.

'Would you be even more of an angel and ring him for me to explain?' she said listlessly.

'Of course I will.' Dinah put the paper back in her bag. 'I bought you a new sponge bag and put some of your stuff in it, but I brought a couple of my own towels, and a nightgown I keep for holidays. All your belongings, and most of Liam's, will have to be dry-cleaned or sent to the laundry. I'll see to it for you. And this shiny little number is a sexy negligée Harry bought me once in a mad, passionate moment. Too skimpy for me long since.'

One of the things Liam adored about Dinah was the way she never tempered her conversation in his company. He whistled when he saw the jade satin dressing gown. 'Gosh, Cat, you never wear anything like that.'

Catrin smiled a little. 'True. Dull old white towelling's more my style—'

'Dull old black towelling now,' he said with relish. 'Can I have some grapes, please?'

Catrin managed a laugh, and thanked Dinah gratefully, but it was an effort to talk, and after her visitors had gone she felt weary, and very conscious of her throbbing head and aching ribs. Her elbows and knees hurt, every breath was still painful, she felt queasy, and she was still in shock from the encounter with Ashe. Other than that she was fine. Her involuntary chuckle turned so quickly to coughing she reminded herself not to laugh again for a while. Not that she was likely to.

Shortly afterwards the night sister came in to introduce herself and chat with Catrin for a moment before doing her rounds, then the patient was left in peace, feeling very vulnerable, and in urgent need of her mother's presence.

'Don't worry, Sister, I don't need you,' said a familiar voice outside. 'I thought I'd check on Miss Hughes before I leave.'

Catrin was seized with sudden panic. The other patients had gone to watch television in a day room, and she was alone in the small ward as Ashe Hope-Ellison approached the bed.

'How are you feeling?' he asked, reaching for her wrist. 'Truthfully,' he added.

'Pretty awful.' She turned her head away, shocked by her reaction to his touch. The feeling intensified as his fingers tightened, no longer the impersonal examination of a doctor.

'Catrin,' he said quietly, and she turned back to him sharply, wincing at the pain in her head.

'You recognised me, then?' she blurted rashly.

'Of course I recognised you!' He glanced over his

shoulder, but there was no one outside in the corridor. He turned back to her, one eyebrow raised. 'Shades of Casablanca.'

'Only this isn't a gin-joint,' said Catrin without warmth.

'No. But of all the hospitals in the entire country it's quite a quirk of fate you were rushed into mine.'

'Not really. I live here.'

His ruler-straight eyebrows drew together in the way she remembered so well. 'For how long?' he asked incredulously.

'About a year.' She looked at him levelly. 'How about you?'

'Six months.'

Catrin turned her head away wearily.

'Are you by any chance curious about the nine years or so before that?' he asked suavely, studying her chart.

'No,' she lied in a whisper, wishing he would go away and leave her in peace. Normally she would have fired a great many questions at him, whether he wanted to answer them or not. But for the moment she was in very real danger of throwing up, all her energies channelled into willing her stomach into submission. To be physically sick in front of Mr Consultant would be the ultimate humiliation. She blenched at the thought.

'What's wrong?' he demanded.

What isn't? she thought drearily.

'Tell me,' he commanded, moving closer.

Catrin breathed in deeply, then began to cough, and

with deft hands he eased her up on the pillows. He gave her some water, watching as she sipped, his eyes intent on hers.

'Tell me what's bothering you, Catrin,' he ordered.

You are, she thought malevolently. 'Silly things, really. I expect my head to hurt, and my chest, but my knees and elbows hurt too. And a few other places I'd rather not mention.'

'All due to your fall. According to the paramedics you were lucky,' said Ashe matter-of-factly. 'What do you remember?'

Catrin thought for a minute, trying hard to concentrate. 'I smelt smoke in the flat,' she said hoarsely. 'My friend Dinah got Liam out while I rang for the fire brigade. Then the kitchen window exploded and I rushed out after the others, but I couldn't see a thing through the smoke in the hallway. I tried to hurry, but I tripped and went hurtling down the stairs, and hit my head. After that nothing.'

Ashe's jaw tightened, and he took her hand again. 'You probably ricocheted off the walls on the way down, but by some miracle you managed to escape fracturing your skull. As it is you've got raw elbows and knees, various bruises, and concussion from the bump on your temple. It could have been a lot worse,' he added curtly.

'Yes,' she said, mortified. 'So I'm told. Sorry to moan.'

'You weren't moaning, Catrin. It was a nightmare experience, and you're still suffering from shock.'

How right he was. Catrin essayed a wobbly smile.

'The worst part was worrying about Liam—' She halted as Sister Lockwood came to join them.

'Is everything all right, Dr Hope-Ellison?' she asked.

'Miss Hughes is just beginning to realise the full extent of her injuries, Sister.' He turned back to Catrin for a moment, smiled at her with fleeting warmth, then wished her a restful night and went out with Sister. Catrin felt limp with reaction, glad Ashe had gone, but her relief was short-lived. After a brief conversation with Sister outside in the corridor he startled Catrin by reappearing at the foot of her bed.

'Catrin,' he said casually, 'who is Liam?'

She stared at him blankly. 'He's my brother.'

'Your brother,' he repeated without inflection. His eyes held hers for a long moment, then he gave her an unsettling smile. 'Of course. Attractive lad. Goodnight.'

When she was finally settled for the night Catrin felt wretched for a variety of reasons. Her entire body aching, and her mind was so full of Ashe she slept very little, and she felt heartily glad when the bustle of a new hospital day began at last.

By mid-morning, Catrin was surrounded with flowers and offerings from friends at the office, and both looked and felt a lot better than the day before. And, though she spent a tense, expectant half-hour before morning rounds, it was Dr Hawkins, the senior Registrar, who headed the little retinue and instructed one of his colleagues to listen to her chest and test her for concussion. There was no sign of Ashe, but to Catrin's dismay she was pronounced unfit to be discharged for at least another day.

Dr Hope-Ellison, she was told, would look in on her at some stage to pronounce her ready to leave, but for today she could relax, too unimportant a patient to require the consultant's personal attention. Not that she wanted it, she thought savagely.

Catrin had plenty of other people eager to pay her attention. In addition to Liam and Dinah during the afternoon, some of her fellow accountants from the firm called in on their way home, and George Duffield, the senior partner who'd given the party, brought his wife in for a short visit during the evening. After they'd gone the tall, elegant figure of Julian Fellowes, complete with extravagant spray of orchids, caused a ripple of interest from her fellow patients as he bent to kiss Catrin.

'Lord, Catrin, I can't apologise enough,' he said remorsefully, plainly horrified at the sight of her. 'But I had the chance of landing another contract. If I'd only got back for the party you wouldn't have gone home early, and this wouldn't have happened.'

'As it happens, I'm very glad I did,' she retorted. 'Liam and Dinah were in the flat, remember.'

But Julian wasn't interested in her little brother, nor in her forthright friend. He was also, Catrin could tell, totally dismayed by the unappetising sight of her with lank hair and black eye, and only too eager to escape as soon as he could.

'We met Julian galloping along the corridor,' said Dinah, as she arrived with Liam.

Catrin smiled wryly. 'Despite your dashing dressing gown, my appearance was obviously very off-putting. And because he also feels vaguely guilty Julian was ready to run after only a minute or two.'

'The man's an idiot,' said Dinah dismissively. 'That rather terrifying sister says you can come home tomorrow afternoon, by the way, once you're given the all-clear. The agency has done wonders with the flat; it's as clean as a whistle. But I suggest you both stay at my place for a while, until you feel more the thing, love.'

'That's very good of you, but we'll manage very well. You've had enough disruption in your life for a bit,' said Catrin firmly.

Liam eyed Dinah anxiously. 'I hope I haven't been a terrible nuisance.'

Dinah gave him a hug. 'Anything but, my dear. You can stay with me any time you like. It's been a pleasure.'

'I've got to go back to school on Thursday,' said Liam glumly. 'The staff are all recovered now.'

'Bad luck,' said Catrin with sympathy. 'Anyway, Mum and Dad will be home next week, and soon after that it's half-term.'

'Besides,' said Dinah slyly, 'your street cred will rocket when you tell the other chaps you escaped from a fire.'

Liam brightened visibly. 'I'll say! Can I have some of your chocolates, Cat?'

'I do feed him,' said Dinah, resigned.

Catrin laughed. 'So do I, but it makes no difference. His stomach's a bottomless pit.'

'I'm growing,' said Liam, munching ecstatically.

'An inch a day by the look of you,' said Dinah. 'Especially your feet. I'm afraid we need a shopping spree for boring black school shoes,' she told Catrin.

Catrin rummaged in her side-table for her wallet, and handed over her bank card. 'Liam, you know the PIN number. If you need more, Dinah, I'll settle up later.'

'Can I use some of it to treat Dinah to lunch?' asked Liam hopefully.

'Good idea,' approved Catrin, then tensed suddenly, her heart thumping as the tall, elegant figure of Dr Hope-Ellison strolled into the ward.

'Hello, again,' he said pleasantly, smiling at Catrin's visitors. 'My name's Hope-Ellison.'

'My friend, Mrs Martin, and my brother Liam,' she said stiffly.

There was an exchange of greetings, after which Liam was obviously impatient to leave.

'Soccer match on TV tonight—Manchester United versus Everton,' he said with relish, then looked guilty. 'It's not on *very* late, Cat.'

She grinned at him. 'Make the most of it. Back to school on Thursday.'

CHAPTER TWO

AFTER they'd gone Ashe picked up her chart and studied it, then asked Catrin a few routine questions.

'I didn't expect to see you today,' she said bluntly. 'They told me you'd be round in the morning to pronounce judgement.'

'It was one of my private clinic days. But I had to come back to the hospital tonight so I thought I'd call in here to see how you are. After all, we were friends once, Catrin—much more than friends, to be accurate.' His eyes met hers, bright with challenge. 'But I'll leave if you object.'

She shrugged. 'I'm not in a position to object.'

There was silence for a moment, with only the usual hospital hum of people passing outside in the corridor, telephones ringing. To the casual observer they were doctor and patient, but after Ashe's deliberate descent into intimacy the tension between them mounted until it lay in the air between them. The silence stretched and grew until Catrin was shaking inside before Ashe broke it.

'You said your brother was going back to school,' he said at last. 'Has he been ill?'

Catrin looked away, unable to bear the piercing blue scrutiny any longer. 'No. Liam's fine, but a flue epidemic mowed down the teaching staff. They had to close his school for a while, so he came to stay with me.'

'He lives with you?'

'Not normally, no. But my mother's away on holiday.'

'Has she been informed of your accident?'

'No.' Catrin forced herself to face him again. 'I'll get a lecture when Mother gets back next week. But I wasn't in any danger—'

'Other than almost breaking your neck in a life-threatening fire,' he put in caustically.

'It was the shoes,' she said, depressed.

'Shoes?' he said, frowning.

'With four-inch gold heels.' Her smile was wry. 'Even in a sale they cost an arm and a leg.'

'They could have cost you a hell of a sight more than that!' he said in a fierce undertone, the calm, professional air suddenly missing. 'Didn't it occur to you to kick the damn things off?'

'My first thought was to get Liam and Dinah out of there,' she returned hotly. 'My shoes were not uppermost in my mind, Dr Hope-Ellison,' she added deliberately.

His face hardened at the formality. 'I see. When you leave here tomorrow, where are you going?'

'Back to my flat. Mrs Martin's had it cleaned professionally.'

He moved closer, frowning. 'Cat, are you sure you're up to coping alone?'

She bit her lip, her heart contracting at the diminutive. 'I doubt if I'll be allowed to do that. Dinah—

Mrs Martin—lives in the flat above. She wants us to stay with her for a while, but I think it's best I get straight back to my own place.'

'Otherwise,' he said intuitively, 'you might never want to go back at all.'

'Exactly.' Catrin looked away and the silence returned, lengthening again to stretch her much-tried nerves. She wanted Ashe to go, to leave her in peace, yet at the same time longed for him to stay, to catch her up in his arms and hold her close and kiss her better. As if he knew what she was thinking Ashe took her hand again, an eye on his watch to show the world he was checking her pulse, and Catrin trembled at his touch and cleared her throat, desperate for something to say. 'My boss insists I take whatever time is necessary to recuperate,' she managed unevenly, 'so I won't try to get back to work for a while.'

'What do you do?' asked Ashe, one of his fingers stroking a throbbing blue vein in her wrist.

'I'm a chartered accountant,' she said hoarsely.

'How impressive!' He laid her hand gently on the sheet, frowning as the hectic colour drained from her face, leaving the bruise livid against her pallor. 'You look tired, Catrin. I'll call a nurse to settle you for the night.'

'Thank you,' she whispered, utterly vanquished by the note of tenderness in his voice.

Ashe eyed her thoughtfully for a moment, then asked, 'By the way, how old is Liam?

Her eyes narrowed. 'He's nine. Why?'

'Just curious. He looks more than that.'

'I know. He's big for his age.' Her one good eye gazed at him speculatively. By now he was sure to have a family of his own, probably a son or two to compare with Liam. But no way was she going to ask.

Ashe stood looking at her for a moment, as though he had other questions to ask, then voices in the corridor heralded the return of Catrin's fellow patients, and with a courteous nod he bade her goodnight.

Catrin watched him go, unsurprised at Ashe's disbelief. Although Liam was a normal boy in every respect he was surprisingly mature, as well as tall for his age. And much as she loved him Catrin wasn't sorry Liam would soon be back in school. In her present feeble condition, he was a complication her life could do without until she felt normal. And at the moment, much as she despised herself for her weakness, 'normal' seemed a long way off.

Next morning there was no sign of Ashe. It fell to Dr Hawkins to discharge her. He gave her a few basic instructions about diet and rest, instructed the nurse to change the dressing on her head wound, and told Catrin to return to Outpatients for removal of the stitches and a general check-up. She thanked him politely, wondering if she'd ever see Ashe again. The sensible part of her hoped not, for several reasons. Just to look at him caused turmoil she'd hoped never to experience again. Besides, he was very different from the Ashe of the brief summer idyll they'd shared so long ago.

'That's a deep frown,' said the nurse. 'Did I hurt you?'

Catrin smiled absently. 'No, of course not.'

'I'll help you get dressed, then you'll be ready when it's time to go home.'

Dinah had already collected some of Catrin's clothes from the dry-cleaners, and brought brown wool trousers and suede boots, and a thick cream sweater with a tangerine silk scarf to knot at the neck for colour. When Catrin was ready, complete with lipstick to match the scarf, Liam's face was bright with relief.

'Gosh, you look better, Cat,' he said happily.

'I'm a lot better. And I'll be better still in my own bed,' she assured him. 'Thanks for volunteering for the sofa, love.'

'Easier to watch television,' he declared, grinning.

Catrin gave her flowers to the other patients, and after farewells and thanks to the nursing staff the trio returned to the nineteenth-century building on the edge of town, where the ground-floor flat was an ugly, gutted reminder of the fire, and the main door was still waiting for a security lock.

Catrin shivered on the way up the smoke-blackened staircase, eyeing the wrought-iron handrail malevolently. It was carved intricately, each newel post crowned with a finial fashioned to represent a different fruit. 'I suppose some of these things are to blame for my fine array of bruises. The pineapple gets my vote for most dangerous, I think.'

Dinah eyed it with dislike. 'Sheer Victorian

whimsy to put a pineapple in Orchard House. Come on. Feet up for you.'

'Wow!' said Liam, as they reached the landing. 'Look at those.'

A basket filled with brilliant blue irises stood outside the door. Dinah whistled as she handed Catrin the card. 'Julian?'

'No,' said Catrin faintly. 'Dr Hope-Ellison. How—how nice of him.'

Dinah's eyes gleamed, but she tactfully refrained from comment. 'Come in at once and sit down. Where shall I put the flowers?'

Catrin subsided on her newly cleaned sofa, looking round at the flat, which, though immaculate, still smelt a little of smoke, mingled with the various cleaning fluids the agency had used. 'In the corner near the window, I suppose, so we don't fall over them.'

'I'll put the kettle on,' said Liam importantly, and went off to the kitchen, whistling.

Dinah gave Catrin a searching look. 'How are you? Really, I mean?'

'As well as can be expected,' Catrin smiled ruefully. 'The big wide world outside the hospital feels a lot bigger than before, somehow.'

'Like leaving the womb,' agreed her friend, then fixed Catrin with a worldly-wise dark eye. 'Tell me to mind my own business, but I've never heard of a consultant who sends flowers to his patients. Something tells me you've met the charismatic Dr Hope-Ellison before.'

'Very briefly. And a long time ago.' Catrin cast a warning eye kitchenwards. 'I'll tell you about it some time.'

'I can't wait!' Dinah looked up, applauding, as Liam reappeared with a tea-tray, tongue between his teeth in intense concentration as he deposited it safely on a small table. He beamed at his sister.

'There you are. No spills—and your favourite biscuits.'

'Who could ask for more?' approved Catrin, touched.

The following afternoon Dinah took Liam swimming, officially as a last fling before school, but in actual fact, as Catrin knew very well, to give her a rest from her exuberant young brother's company in the confines of the flat.

'I owe you,' she told Dinah, as Liam shot out onto the landing.

'Haven't had so much fun in years,' said her friend, then yelled, 'Steady on, Liam. Watch out for the killer pineapple!'

Catrin tried lying on the sofa for a while, as bidden, watching an old black and white weepy movie on TV, but she quickly tired of that, along with the novel she tried to read afterwards. She was glad of the interruption when the phone rang, expecting to hear from Julian. But her caller was Ashe.

'How are you feeling?' he asked, the voice so familiar, and so disturbing, that the years rolled away, leaving her vulnerable to the never-forgotten charm of it.

'Better,' she said, determinedly brisk. 'I'm glad you rang.'

'Why?'

'So I could thank you for the exquisite flowers. I didn't like to contact the hospital.'

'I'm glad you liked them. But I didn't ring to be thanked.'

'Why did you ring?' she asked curiously.

'Is it beyond the bounds of possibility that I just wanted to talk to you?' He paused. 'I took your number from your hospital records. I hope you don't object.'

'No.' On the contrary, she was so pleased she made her voice deliberately cool in case he could tell.

'Good. As an old friend,' he added deliberately, 'I was concerned about your progress. Any problems, Catrin?'

'The head aches a bit, and I don't feel very energetic, but I'm a fairly sensible type, Ashe. I'll make sure I do all the right things to get back to normal.'

'You weren't always so sensible,' he said abruptly, and colour flooded Catrin's face at the note in his voice.

'Neither were you,' she retorted hotly, and had the satisfaction of hearing him breathe in sharply.

'Catrin—' he began urgently, then halted. 'There's something I want to ask you,' he went on, his voice in control again.

She swallowed, breathing fast. 'Yes? What is it?'

'I was wondering where Liam's school is.'

Catrin came down to earth with a jolt. 'Liam's school?' she said coldly, when she had herself in hand. 'It's in Shropshire. Why?'

'How is he getting back?'

'The same way he came,' she said curtly. 'One of Liam's classmates lives about ten miles out of town. His father gave Liam a lift here last week, and offered to collect him tomorrow for the return trip. Why?'

'It occurred to me that you couldn't drive him in your present state, so I thought I'd volunteer my services.'

'How very kind,' said Catrin acidly, 'but quite unnecessary. I wouldn't dream of troubling you.'

'Catrin, don't hang up,' he said quickly, sensing her withdrawal. 'I need to talk to you.'

Catrin had been certain Ashe had rung because he wanted to see her again, and now she was mortified, both by her mistake, and the fact that she wanted to see him again. Which was out of the question.

'Catrin?' Ashe demanded. 'Are you there?'

'Yes,' she said with hostility. 'I'm here. But I don't need—or want—to talk to you, Ashe.' She put the phone down quickly before she forgot principles and hurt pride and agreed to anything he wanted. When the phone rang again immediately, Catrin took the receiver off the handset, placed it on the table with a click and went off to have a bath.

Catrin was unprepared for the loneliness she felt when Liam had gone back to school. With the flat to herself it was difficult to control her new paranoia about electrical appliances and light switches, and anything and everything that might remotely cause a fire. It was silly. Immature. Lightning never struck twice. She tried to convince herself of it over and over again, but it was impossible. And she had nightmares. Not every night, but enough to make her dread going to bed. Sleep was difficult anyway, because she lay awake for hours on end, thinking about Ashe. By day she could occupy herself in various ways to keep thoughts of him at bay. But at night she was helpless against the memories she'd kept firmly locked away for the past ten years.

Catrin kept her answer machine on permanently, so she could monitor her calls. Ashe rang twice after his first phone call, but after no response from Catrin he gave up, long before his flowers were dead. And Julian rang from whichever part of the Continent he was harassing for more orders for his software firm, promising to come and see her the moment he was back in the UK.

A week after her discharge from hospital, on the day she was due to go back to Outpatients, Catrin was feeling a lot better—other than her reluctance to run into Ashe again. Not that she would, of course. The lordly consultant would no doubt delegate this particular patient to someone else. But whichever underling had the pleasure of unstitching her she wasn't looking forward to the process.

When Catrin arrived at the hospital the outpatients department was full, as usual, and she settled down with a book to a lengthy wait. When her name was called at last Catrin was sent to a cubicle where a young doctor removed the stitches with minimum fuss, to her relief, assured her the scar would hardly show, then directed her along the corridor to a door at the end.

'Just knock and go in. My boss wants to check on you before we let you go,' he said cheerfully, and called for the next patient.

Catrin bit her lip, then squared her shoulders. Best to get it over with. She knocked and went into the consulting room, but instead of Ashe she found Dr Hawkins waiting to pronounce her fit.

Fool, she thought bitterly, as she left the hospital. One minute she was annoyed because she expected to see Ashe, the next minute shattered because it was Dr Hawkins instead. Time she pulled herself together, went back to work, got on with her nice, tidy life. As she marched past the staff car park a car glided out to stop in front of her.

'Hello, Catrin,' said Ashe, opening the passenger door. 'I'm going your way. Can I give you a lift?'

She cast an eye at the line of vehicles forming behind them, thought better of refusing and got in the car. 'Thank you.'

'So how did it go?' he asked, his attention on the stream of traffic he was joining.

'My stitches are out and Dr Hawkins has pronounced me fit, so it went very well, thank you. I'll go back to work next week.'

Ashe gave her a brief sidelong glance. 'You look better, Cat. The bruise faded quickly.'

'Yes. I can just about face myself in a mirror again,' she said, gazing fixedly through the window.

'You never returned my calls.'

Catrin shot a startled look at him. 'No.'

'Why not?'

Her eyes flashed coldly. 'I would have thought that was obvious.'

'Tell me anyway,' he commanded.

'Oh, come on, Ashe!' she said scornfully. 'You know perfectly well. Did you really expect me to be overjoyed to see you again?'

His jaw tightened. 'Overjoyed or not, Catrin, you felt some reaction. You can't hide a pulse-rate from a doctor.' His swift, sidelong glance glittered. 'You were no more immune to my touch than I was to yours. And very unprofessional it made me feel, I assure you. Sister Lockwood was beginning to eye me suspiciously. I'm not in the habit of making extra visits to patients unless called in.'

'So why was *I* honoured?'

Without answering, Ashe drove through the park gates and stopped in the deserted car park before turning to look Catrin in the eye. 'You know damn well why. The same reason why I couldn't keep away from you all those years ago.' He reached out a hand and took hold of her wrist, his fingers finding the pulse that throbbed there.

Catrin stared down at the capable, long-fingered hand, remembering all too vividly how the touch of it had once set her on fire. And, unfortunately, still did. She withdrew her hand firmly. 'It was a long time ago, Ashe. We had quite a little fire going for a while, I agree. But it went out.'

'It could be rekindled, Catrin.'

'Definitely not.' She bent her head, refusing to look at him.

'Why not?'

'For reasons many and varied,' she said succinctly.

'On both sides,' he said grimly, then his voice softened. 'Some things are still the same, Catrin. You still hide behind your hair.'

'Normally I wear it pinned back,' she said coolly, and raised her head with hauteur. 'But at the moment I prefer to hide the scar.'

'And,' he went on, as though she hadn't spoken, 'you still bite your bottom lip until all I can think of is wanting to kiss it better—'

'I can walk home from here,' said Catrin in sudden alarm, and wrenched free of his clasp to rattle at the door handle. 'Please let me out, Ashe.'

'My dear girl,' he drawled, releasing the central locking system. 'Calm down. I'll drive you home right now if you'll tell me where you live.'

'Thank you,' said Catrin, deflated, and gave him directions.

When Ashe drew up outside the flat he eyed the gutted ground floor grimly. 'My God, Catrin, you were lucky. It's a miracle the entire building didn't go up.'

'A thought which keeps me awake at nights,' she

agreed lightly. 'Thank you for bringing me home, Ashe.'

With the inevitable dark suit Ashe was wearing a blue shirt which matched his eyes, and as he turned to look at her Catrin was suddenly seized with the desire to melt in his arms, to see if the magic was still there.

'Catrin,' he said huskily, his eyes kindling, and she looked away hastily.

'Lucky for me you happened to be in the hospital car park. I didn't feel like a trip home on the bus.'

His laugh raised the hairs on her spine. 'I didn't ''happen'' to be there, Cat. I checked to find out when your name cropped up on Dick Hawkins' list, and lay in wait for you.'

'Did you really? You needn't have troubled,' she said angrily. 'Goodbye, Ashe!'

And before he could say any more she was out of the car and on her way to the smoke-blackened door of Orchard House, just as Dinah arrived, her face bright with curiosity as she recognised the man in the car.

'Well, well,' she commented, as she went inside with Catrin. 'I assume the dashing doctor brought you home. How did the check-up go?'

'Fine. Back to work on Monday.'

Dinah paused outside Catrin's door. 'How about sharing a meal tonight? I'll cook something.'

'I'd love to.'

'There's a price, Catrin,' Dinah warned, smiling. 'I

can't stand the suspense any longer. If you don't tell me your little story soon I'll expire with curiosity.'

Catrin laughed, and held up her hands in surrender. 'Oh, all right. Done. In return for your special pasta, I'll gladly sing for my supper.'

And, she thought later, on her way up to Dinah's flat, seeing Ashe again had brought it all back so vividly it would be a relief to talk about him to someone at last. Now that he was back in her life again she couldn't stop thinking about him anyway. Not only thinking, but remembering. The brief, halcyon time they'd spent together was as clear in her mind as though it had happened yesterday, instead of ten years ago.

CHAPTER THREE

THE small cove formed a perfect sun-trap. Catrin lay in her favourite crevice in the rocks as usual that fateful day, eyes closed, revelling in the warm, morning sunlight. Suddenly her retreat was invaded and she shot upright in startled, laughing protest as a wet, shaggy intruder launched itself on her, licking her face in ecstatic greeting.

'Poll, get off, you monster!' Catrin sat up, fending off the hotel retriever, then patted him to show she wasn't annoyed. 'Good boy. Heavens, you're a mess—covered in sand. And you're not supposed to come down here on your own.'

A man came racing up in hot pursuit. 'I'm very sorry,' he said breathlessly. 'I didn't see you there. I hope he didn't frighten you.'

Catrin looked up into an attractive, haggard face, and smiled. 'Not in the least. Poll and I are old friends.' She reached for her shirt and put it on, gesturing towards the hotel perched on the cliff overlooking the cove. 'Are you staying up there?' she asked politely as the dog settled himself beside her.

'Yes. I arrived yesterday.' The man looked at her questioningly. 'If you and Poll are such old friends why haven't I seen you before?'

'I'm a local, not a guest. With special dispensation

to use the private beach.' She smoothed the dog's glossy damp head. 'The hotel manager knows my family.'

She kept her eyes on the dog's head as the stranger let himself down on the sand, his back to a rock. He stretched out his legs with a sigh, staring out to sea.

'I'll go away if you prefer,' he offered, after a minute or two of silence.

'You've more right to be here than me,' she said shyly, and smiled. 'Besides, Poll wants to stay, by the look of him.'

The dog was fast asleep, his head against her bare thigh, and the man looked down at him, then up into Catrin's face, his slate-blue eyes gleaming below flopping hair as glossy and black as Poll's.

'Then I take it I have permission to do the same? What's your name?'

'Catrin.'

He stripped off his white sweatshirt and lay back comfortably, wearing only a pair of khaki shorts, flustering his companion not a little. 'Hello, Catrin. I'm Ashe with an "e",' he said, closing fatigue-smudged eyes.

'First or last name?'

'Just Ashe—my first name is so gross I never use it.' He opened an eye and looked at her. 'So what do you do, Catrin?'

'At the moment I'm marking time. Waiting.'

'For what exactly?'

'Exam results.' The sun was hot, and she wanted to take off her shirt again, but couldn't quite bring herself to do it. Which was irritating. She'd never suffered from shyness before.

'And when you get these exam results?' he prompted.

'If the grades are good enough I'll go on to university in October.'

'Good for you.' He yawned a little, and apologised. 'Lack of sleep, not boredom, Catrin.' He smiled at her warmly.

'Have you been ill?' she asked gently.

The smile vanished. 'Why do you ask?'

Catrin retreated. 'You look tired, that's all.'

'Sorry. Didn't mean to bite your head off.' He reached out a hand and touched hers fleetingly. 'I'm a lowly hospital doctor, hence the circles under the eyes and the air of chronic exhaustion. In three weeks I go to a new job at a big teaching hospital, and in the meantime I've come here for a while to eat, sleep and recharge my batteries.' He paused, a straight black eyebrow raised. 'You obviously find that surprising. Why?'

She shrugged. 'It's such a quiet place to choose.'

'I like quiet. It's a refreshing change. And I didn't fancy a more reliable foreign sun,' he said with a hint of bitterness, then looked at her in silence for a while. 'Catrin,' he said at last.

'Yes?'

'Take the hat off, please—and the sunglasses. I'd like to see your face.'

She looked at him uncertainly, but did as he asked, unaware that her slow, reluctant removal of both hat and dark glasses was as innocently sensual as a strip-tease to the man watching. She shook out her long brown hair and turned to face him.

'Green eyes, like a cat,' he said very softly. 'Shall I call you Cat?'

'If you like.' She put the glasses and the white cotton hat back on, needing their protection. His direct blue gaze unsettled her. No man had ever looked at her like that before, and suddenly she was wary. She picked up her book deliberately, and with one swift movement Ashe stood up, gathered up his sweatshirt and clicked his fingers at the dog.

'Right, Apollo, time to go.' He smiled down at Catrin. 'Do you come here every day?'

'No, not every day.'

He waited for her to go on, but Catrin said nothing, and after a moment he shrugged. 'Perhaps I'll see you again.'

She smiled noncommittally, startled at how much she wanted to tell him she'd be there tomorrow if he wanted. But caution held her tongue. 'Perhaps. It was nice meeting you.'

Ashe laughed. 'Such a polite little thing. It was very nice meeting you, too.'

Catrin watched him stroll across the beach with the dog, admiring the musculature of his lean back and long bare legs, the thatch of black hair in need of a trim. She saw him pause to talk for a moment as he reached a group of hotel guests sunning themselves on deckchairs on the sand, and noted the way female heads turned as he leapt up the steps cut into the cliff to give easy access to the hotel.

Dr Ashe, Catrin decided, had more than his share of the mysterious male quality which turned female heads. She sighed irritably and got up. She had meant to stay all day, but if she did Ashe would think she'd hung about on the off chance of seeing him again. She packed her belongings in her rucksack and slung it over her shoulders, then picked her way over the rocks to the steep, rarely used track which wound up from her end of the beach. Panting in the bright sunlight, glad of her hat against the glare, Catrin climbed the path to the clifftop with the speed of long practice, and made for the field where the farmer allowed her to hide her bicycle in a copse of stunted, windblown trees.

On the ride home she found herself thinking of her morning encounter to the exclusion of all else, taken aback to find that for the first time in her life she wished she were prettier.

Catrin had rarely given much thought to her looks. She was boyishly thin, her full mouth a shade too wide for her narrow face. At the moment her skin was tanned, but in winter it tended to sallowness, and, although her hair was thick and shining, she suddenly wished it was something more glamorous than ordinary dark brown. Even the eyes which Ashe had thought were green merely echoed the shirt pulled on over her swimsuit. Their colour changed according to what she wore, or her mood, or her state of health.

Up to now Catrin had never worried about her lack

of voluptuous curves, or conventional prettiness. She was popular with both males and females of her own age, but had never had any one particular boyfriend, nor wanted one, and felt bored and embarrassed when excited girlfriends confided personal secrets about theirs. Yet in one brief conversation Dr Ashe had made her aware of sensations and reactions totally outside her experience. Arrested development, she decided in amusement.

Home to the Hughes family was a solid stone house with several acres of land once used as a smallholding. When Tom Hughes had inherited it from his father he'd installed irrigation, created a market garden, and soon had a success on his hands. People came from miles around to buy vegetables, bedding plants and perennials, and pick their own strawberries and soft fruits. And his wife had worked alongside him to make the business a success. Now Julia Hughes managed it alone.

Catrin went swiftly through the empty house and up to her room to change into jeans, then back down to the large, glass-roofed sale hall where her mother was manning one of the check-out points.

'I'll take over,' she offered, and Julia smiled affectionately.

'Had enough sunbathing, darling?'

'For now. Have a break, you look tired.' Catrin slid into the seat and smiled at the first customer. 'Hello. Sorry to keep you waiting.'

Catrin went down early to breakfast next morning to offer her services again. Her mother, who had been up at the crack of dawn to check on the irrigation system, looked up, startled, from the letter she was reading, and put it in her pocket, her cheeks flushed. 'You needn't, love. I've got plenty of staff in today. Go and lie on the beach again. It's a shame to waste this weather. You deserve the rest after all that studying.'

Catrin assured her mother the weather was due to hold for some time. 'I'll go back to the beach tomorrow. Take some time off yourself. You deserve a rest now and then, too.'

Catrin was determined to keep well away from the beach for one day, at least, as self-discipline—just in case the charismatic Dr Ashe thought she was turning up solely to meet him again.

The morning after that, however, Catrin made more sandwiches than usual and put them in a cooler bag, added fruit, poured orange juice into an insulated flask, and packed it all into her rucksack with her usual book, towel and sun-cream.

As she cycled towards the cove Catrin found she was tingling with excitement. Over a mere man, she mocked herself. But it was true. At the prospect of meeting Ashe again she felt exhilarated, anticipation fizzing along her veins like champagne.

Catrin hid her bicycle and clambered down the narrow track. She picked her way across the rocks to the familiar crevice, took off her rucksack and laid her towel down, then stripped off shorts and shirt and made them into a pillow for her head before anointing herself with sun-cream.

'Can I help?' said the voice she'd been hoping to hear, and she looked up to see Ashe grinning at her appreciatively, the remembered gleam in his eyes.

'Hello.' She smiled, and sat down on the towel, putting the bottle away in her rucksack. 'How are you today?'

'All the better for seeing you, Catrin. May I join you?'

She nodded matter-of-factly, hoping he couldn't hear her heart banging against her ribs. 'Where's Poll?'

'I left him behind—three's a crowd.' He frowned suddenly, and knelt on the sand in front of her. 'Your eyes!' he said, astonished. 'They're blue today.'

She flushed. 'They change according to the clothes I wear.'

'Chameleon eyes,' he said softly, and smiled. 'What happens when you wear nothing at all?'

With a look of distaste she turned away, put on her glasses and the sunhat, then opened her book.

Ashe touched her hand in swift remorse. 'Cat, I'm sorry. Don't freeze me off.'

'Then don't talk like that,' she snapped.

'I won't again, I promise.' He sat down with his back against the same rock, legs stretched out in front of him. 'Where were you yesterday? I missed you.'

Catrin's heart missed a beat. 'I was working.'

'Studying?'

'No. I do part-time work in the holidays.'

He sighed. 'Heigh-ho, and there was I thinking I'd have company on the beach every day.'

'Plenty of people over there on the hotel deck-chairs,' she pointed out.

'None of them as appealing as you, Cat.' His face set. 'My fellow hotel guests are all couples of varying descriptions. I'm the only loner on the list.'

'Do you have to pay a lot more for that?'

'In sorrow or in money?'

Catrin chuckled. 'I know the hotel's expensive, and all the rooms are doubles, so I thought you'd have to pay accordingly.'

'I do.' His face hardened, making him look older. 'One way and another I'm paying through the nose.'

Catrin changed the subject hastily. 'What did you do yesterday? You've acquired quite a tan since I saw you last.'

'I hung about on the beach all day, waiting for you to turn up.' He gave her a soulful blue glance.

She raised an eyebrow, her silence eloquent with disbelief.

'It's the truth,' he assured her seriously. 'I was doing the same this morning. Why do you think I materialised so quickly the moment you appeared?'

'I assumed you were on the beach already.'

'I was. But I was waiting in the wrong place. I didn't know there was a path over this end.' He frowned. 'Are you sure it's safe? It looks hellish steep from here, strictly for mountain goats.'

'It zigzags about a bit on its way up. It's not as bad as it looks,' she assured him.

Ashe looked unconvinced. 'Why don't you use the hotel path?'

'I prefer to keep a low profile. Besides,' she added, 'it's the quickest way home for me.'

'Does your father know you use the path?'

'My father died eighteen months ago. Don't be embarrassed,' she added quickly. 'You weren't to know.'

He put out a hand to touch hers. 'I'm sorry, Catrin. You miss him?'

'Very much. But don't let's talk about it. Tell me about life as a hospital doctor.'

Ashe was a good raconteur. He told her hilarious anecdotes from his student days, gave her lurid warnings about the male of the species when she became a student herself, and asked about her own life. Catrin found it remarkably easy to talk to him, aware of a rapport she'd never felt with anyone before.

He agreed to share her lunch on condition that he brought a picnic down from the hotel the following day, and Catrin made no effort to pretend she might not come.

The only flaw in the entire day was a visit from Mrs Marshall, the hotel manager, during their meal. She came towards them with Apollo on a lead, bringing a message for Ashe, who jumped to his feet, frowning.

'I believe it's urgent, Doctor,' she announced, after a cool smile at Catrin. 'My staff are all busy in the dining room so I brought it myself.'

'Thank you,' said Ashe shortly. 'Don't go away, Catrin. I'll be back.'

As he sprinted away across the sand Mrs Marshall asked if Catrin's results were out, sent her regards to

Julia, then gave in to the dog's importuning and walked back across the beach.

Catrin pulled a face. Mrs Marshall obviously disapproved of guests fraternising with locals, and Catrin mentioned it to Ashe when he returned a few minutes later.

'Don't let it worry you,' he said firmly. 'Sorry about that. Where were we?'

'Not bad news, I hope,' she said diffidently, worried by the look in his eyes.

He shook his head, shaking off the change of mood with it. 'Nothing to worry about.'

When Catrin left Ashe later she made no demur when he took it for granted she'd come to the beach next morning. After the first day in Ashe's company she was secretly only too eager to spend as much time with him as he wanted, and had to force herself to be a few minutes late to salve her own pride. After a second day of nonstop conversation and sunbathing, punctuated by a swim now and then, and a lunchbreak, she began to feel they'd known each other for ever. And when Catrin began gathering her things together in the evening for the trip home, Ashe insisted on carrying her rucksack up the cliff path for her.

'Please!' she said, scarlet to the roots of her hair. 'There are people watching. I feel conspicuous.'

'Most of them have been watching us all day,' he said, grinning. 'Why not let them see what a gentleman I am? I'll come straight back down, I promise, once I've seen you safely to your bicycle.'

Nothing she could say would deter him, and Catrin used the climb to think quickly. When they arrived at the clifftop, Ashe complaining bitterly about his lack of fitness, he walked to the field with her, and only handed over the rucksack when she was balanced on her bicycle, ready to ride home.

'I've enjoyed my day,' he told her. 'Where, exactly, do you live?'

'A mile or so away; it's not far,' she said, deliberately vague. Ashe was someone to keep separate from her normal life, even from her mother. In a week or so he would be gone. There was no point in introducing him to Julia.

Ashe touched a hand to her flushed cheek. 'You don't want to tell me,' he said indulgently. 'All right, Miss Mystery. You keep your secrets; I keep mine.' His eyes shadowed for a moment, then he smiled quickly. 'See you in the morning.'

Catrin looked at him. 'I don't fancy providing more entertainment for the hotel guests.'

His eyes narrowed. 'Does that mean you've had enough of my company?'

'No. Which,' she added, flushing even more, 'you know very well.'

'I certainly hoped you hadn't.' He smiled. 'So let's go somewhere else. I'll pick you up in the car—'

'No,' Catrin said swiftly. 'Let me drive *you*, instead. I know all the beaches round here, or castles if you prefer, or museums—' She stopped short suddenly, wondering if she'd taken too much for granted, and Ashe squeezed her hand in swift reassurance.

'I'd like nothing better, Cat. Will you come for me at the hotel?'

'No way! Mrs Marshall would put a blight on the day. I'll pick you up right here at eleven—'

'Ten would be better!'

'Eleven,' she said firmly, then grinned at him. 'Though I'd better warn you I only passed my test a month ago.'

'Now she tells me,' he groaned in mock-terror. 'OK. You ignore my chattering teeth, and I'll ignore the crashing gears.'

'Cheek! I never crash my gears.' Catrin smiled at him, gave him a jaunty little wave, and rode off, aware in every fibre that Ashe was watching her out of sight.

At home, Catrin prepared a salad and sliced the remains of a cold chicken, and had a meal ready by the time her mother was free to eat.

'How lovely,' sighed Julia, sitting at the small table Catrin had laid outside in their private garden. 'I shall miss this when you've gone off to university, darling.'

'Which bothers me a lot,' said Catrin, once they'd begun to eat. 'It's high time the estate agent found a buyer for this place, Mother. You've had it for sale for ages, and it's too much for you on your own— you look exhausted.' She bit her lip. 'I ought to have stayed home today to help out.'

'Certainly not,' said Julia firmly. 'I'll be glad of you at the weekend, as usual, but in the week there are more than enough people to cope. And who knows? A buyer may turn up any day, offering the full asking price.' Her eyes, colourless with fatigue, dwelt with pleasure on her tanned, glowing daughter. 'Enjoy your youth while you can. Have you had a good day?'

'Actually, I met someone,' said Catrin, helping herself to more salad. 'Just a boy on holiday, but he's rather nice. I thought I'd show him around a bit tomorrow, now I've got my very own car.'

Her mother looked startled. 'Why, yes, love, of course. Bring him back afterwards for a meal, if you like.'

Which meant Julia Hughes would like to see exactly what kind of 'boy' her daughter had befriended.

Catrin shook her head, laughing. 'And terrify the poor bloke? No way. It's not that sort of thing. I promise I'll be as pure as the driven snow, Mother dear.'

'It's not you I'm worried about,' said Julia dryly.

'I'm driving, remember. If he makes a pass he walks back!'

Catrin had never deceived her mother before. But she passionately wanted to keep Ashe to herself, unwilling to share him with anyone, least of all Julia. Warning bells would clamour in her mother's brain after only one look at the haggard charm of Dr Ashe.

When Catrin arrived at the rendezvous next day, in the small, second-hand car Julia had given her for her birthday, Ashe was waiting for her, dressed in jeans and one of his white sweatshirts, his hair lifting in the breeze coming off the sea. He slid into the car beside her, stowed a holdall in the back seat, then planted a kiss on her cheek before fastening his seat belt.

'Good morning, Cat. You're late.'

'Only five minutes.' She drove off carefully, concentrating hard on a smooth gear change to hide her response to his caress.

'It seemed longer than that. I thought perhaps you'd changed your mind.'

She gave him a reproving look. 'I said I would come. I don't drive very fast, that's all. Where would you like to go?'

'Wherever you want to take me.' Ashe slanted a glittering, black-lashed look at her. 'Though my preference is a secluded beach somewhere, preferably near a pub where I can buy you lunch.'

Catrin chose a tiny beach several miles away, on a route she knew well enough to be able to chat happily with Ashe while she was driving. Eventually she turned into the car park of the Weavers' Arms, and told him the pub did a reasonable lunch. It also provided her with a place to park without making a mess of it.

Ashe relieved her of her rucksack as they left the car, slung it over his shoulders, and took her hand in his as they strolled along the narrow lane to the cliff path. 'So where's the beach?'

'About a mile away. I'm afraid it's a bit of a scramble down the cliff to it, but it's never crowded.'

Ashe whistled incredulously when they came to the top of the track. 'You mean you really expect me to shin down there? Are you trying to kill me?' he demanded, peering over the edge.

'Coward! Follow me. I won't let you fall.'

He growled menacingly, and started after her down the steep path, which was treacherous with loose shale and worn away in places, and Catrin laughed with exhilaration, taunting Ashe as he complained volubly every step of the way. The vertiginous, overgrown bends gave way eventually to large boulders, then to smaller rocks which ringed a small, deserted inlet of sand.

'You were right!' he panted, coming up behind her. 'Not a soul in sight. Why does that surprise me, I wonder?'

'This particular cove is only uncovered at certain times,' she told him. 'When the tide's in it comes right up to the boulders back there. They don't make for very comfortable sunbathing.'

'I wish I'd brought a picnic again now,' he grumbled, as Catrin laid her towel down on the sand. 'I'll never make it back up that obstacle course for lunch.'

'In which case it's a good thing I brought lunch myself—'

'I wanted to take you out for a meal.' His eyes narrowed dangerously. 'But you thought I'd never make it back up there, I suppose. I'm not that unfit!'

'Good,' she said, unmoved, 'because we have to get back up there some time.' She took off her shirt and slid out of her jeans. 'Sit down and get your breath back and you'll soon think it was worth the effort.'

Ashe stripped off his outer clothes, took a towel from his holdall and stretched out full length on the sand beside her. 'Do you bring male companions here often?' he enquired affably as she smoothed sun-cream over her skin.

'No. Why?'

'I thought maybe it was part of the plan. Exhaust the guy, then he doesn't get out of hand at the sight of you in that very fetching swimsuit.'

Catrin looked at him levelly. 'If I think that's likely to happen I don't go out with the ''guy'' in the first place.'

Ashe gazed back for a long moment, then nodded. 'Message received, Catrin.'

They lay in companionable silence for a long time, savouring the peace and privacy of the little cove, with only the gulls wheeling overhead for company.

'This,' breathed Ashe with pleasure, 'is exactly what I need.'

Catrin took off her sunglasses to look at him. 'Peace and quiet?'

He turned his head, the slate-blue eyes shadowed. 'When I came I was stressed out, tired, at odds with the world.'

Catrin turned towards him, propping her chin on one elbow. 'And now?'

'And now, after only a few days, I feel better. The weather's marvellous for once, the hotel's a relaxed sort of place, but best of all I've found you.' He smiled, and shook himself, as though ridding himself of a burden. 'You're very restful company, Catrin.'

'Sounds dull,' she retorted, turning back to lie flat.

'Anything but!' He put out a hand to hold hers. 'How old *are* you, Cat?'

'Eighteen. Just. How old are you?'

'Ten years more than that.'

Catrin said nothing, and he tugged on her hand.

'You're supposed to say "you don't look it".'

'Am I? Sorry.'

Ashe laughed, and rolled over to lie on his stomach, his chin on his clasped hands. 'You're always so composed, little Cat.'

Catrin was pleased he thought so. Lying so close to his semi-nude, tanned body, she secretly felt anything but. 'Do you know many girls my age, Dr Ashe?'

'No,' he said after a moment. 'I suppose I don't.'

'I thought not!'

He laughed. 'Definitely none like you, Cat.' He heaved himself up to a sitting position. 'And, idyllic though this may be, my stomach just gave a very unmannerly rumble. Is there really something to eat in that bag of yours?'

They ate rolls filled with crisp bacon and lettuce, accompanied by ripe tomatoes and a hunk of cheese, and fruit juice from Catrin's insulated flask.

Ashe eyed her in remorse. 'No wonder you were late if you were putting all this together.'

'I didn't. I called in at the local bakery and bought it all there,' she assured him. 'Except the tomatoes and apples. Plenty of those at home.'

'Then you must let me pay—' he began, but her eyes flashed coldly.

'Certainly not.'

'But, Cat, be reasonable, my intention was to treat you to a meal today.'

'That's different,' she said stiffly, packing away the remains of their meal.

He caught her hands. 'Cat, don't. I wouldn't offend you for the world. In fact—' He stopped suddenly, his hands tightening as his eyes locked with hers. He leaned towards her involuntarily and colour rose in Catrin's face in a slow, delectable tide.

Ashe swallowed and dropped her hands like hot coals. 'When our lunch has gone down,' he said hoarsely, turning away, 'we'll go for a swim.'

'Good idea,' agreed Catrin, heart pounding.

'What shall we do tomorrow?'

'I can't come tomorrow.'

He shot a hostile, narrowed glance at her. 'Because I almost overstepped the mark just then?'

Catrin shook her head matter-of-factly. 'Of course not. I'm working tomorrow.'

Ashe scowled. 'All *day*?'

'Until six.'

'Then let me take you out to dinner afterwards instead,' he said urgently.

She looked at him for a moment, then nodded. 'All right.'

'Don't overwhelm me with enthusiasm.'

'Touchy! I'd love to have dinner with you, Dr Ashe. Is that better?'

'Somewhat.'

They lay in silence for a while, both of them drowsy after the meal, but eventually Ashe grew restless and pulled Catrin to her feet to run down into the sea, and for half an hour they swam and splashed each other and behaved as though they were both teenagers. Afterwards they returned to dry out in the sun, and talked for a while, until at last Catrin felt her eyes grow heavy, and she yawned and settled down with her hat over her eyes.

'Wake up, Sleeping Beauty,' whispered a voice in her ear, and she stirred drowsily, running the tip of her tongue over her lips, then felt Ashe's mouth on hers, gently at first, followed by a firmer, coaxing pressure which parted her lips. Catrin gasped, and Ashe raised his head instantly, guilt in his eyes. 'Sorry. I was afraid you'd burn if I let you sleep longer.'

But she *was* burning! Which, Catrin told herself fiercely, served her right for playing with fire.

CHAPTER FOUR

'I TRIED calling your name, even tugging a toe,' said Ashe lightly. He pulled on his jeans, gesturing towards the sea. 'You were out for the count. And if we don't move soon we'll need a helicopter to get out of here.'

Catrin shot up to see the tide coming in at an alarming rate. In minutes she was dressed and their bags were packed, and with Ashe at her heels she was toiling up the track, which seemed twice as steep on the way up. When they reached the top at last Ashe flung down his bag, shrugged off Catrin's rucksack and flopped down full length on the short turf, breathing hard. She slumped beside him, smiling apologetically.

'Sorry. I haven't been here in years—I'd forgotten how steep it is. The path's obviously not used much these days. It used to be in better condition.'

'So did I,' Ashe gasped, glaring up at her. 'I'm supposed to be here for a rest, remember.'

'Never mind,' she said cheerfully. 'You can go back to the hotel for a long bath and a nice sleep, followed by a delicious dinner.'

'Attractive programme,' he said, still breathless. 'Only one thing wrong with it.'

'What's that?'

'I'll be doing it all alone.' His eyes met hers, and he smiled crookedly. 'I'm not really sorry about the kiss, by the way. It was sneaky, but very sweet. To me, anyway.'

Catrin shrugged. 'It certainly woke me up, which was the object of the exercise. Good thing I wasn't there alone.'

Ashe sprang up and yanked her to her feet, rather belying his melodramatic exhaustion. 'You never go there alone, surely!'

'No.'

'Promise me you never will,' he said fiercely.

Catrin eyed him in surprise. 'All right. Calm down, Doctor.'

Ashe relaxed, shrugging. 'I had a sudden vision of you losing your footing on your own, miles from anywhere, cut off—' He shivered. 'What time shall I call for you tomorrow night?'

Catrin stared down at the toe of her sneaker, thinking hard as she scuffed it in the dust. 'If you drive from the hotel for a mile or so along the road to Haverfordwest there's a crossroads with a postbox. I'll be there at eight.'

Ashe eyed her in amusement. 'Very clandestine! How are you explaining away the time you spend with me?'

'I told my mother I'd met a boy who was holidaying here for a few days.' Catrin smiled demurely. 'Which is the gospel truth, except for the "boy" part!'

'Cheeky baggage!' he growled. 'Race you back to the pub.'

* * *

Catrin's high spirits did not go unremarked next day by her mother, nor by the staff at the market garden. And despite a very busy day, helping out with enthusiasm wherever she was needed, she felt on top of the world when she finished work that Saturday night.

'Are you taking the car?' asked Julia, when she came into the house later.

'No. Ashe is picking me up in his.'

'Here?' Julia looked alarmed. 'Why didn't you say so? I look a mess—'

'Not here,' said Catrin firmly. 'I'm walking up to the crossroads. He's meeting me there.'

Julia Hughes gave her daughter an accusing look. 'Are you ashamed of me, by any chance?'

Catrin looked dismayed. 'Of *course* not. Believe me, Mother, when the time comes I'll be only too happy to bring some nice man home in grand traditional manner. But this is just a boy on holiday. He'll be gone next week. But you needn't worry,' she added, grinning, 'he's perfectly respectable.'

Her mother sighed. 'I do hope so, darling. You look gorgeous tonight. The boy doesn't know how honoured he is. It isn't often I see you in a dress.'

Catrin's leaf-green lawn dress had been bought to attend a wedding earlier in the summer, otherwise she would have been hard-pressed for suitable garb to match the careless elegance of Dr Ashe. Her usual clothes ran to jeans and trousers, and skirts so brief they sent her mother's blood pressure up. The dress, however, was long and filmy, with a neckline scooped just low enough to show off her tan without causing parental concern.

Ashe's look of appreciation made it clear her efforts had not been in vain. And she was flattered to see he had obviously been waiting some time at the cross-roads, even though she was five minutes early.

'Cat, you look good enough to eat,' he said fervently, leaning over to open the car door. 'It's hard to believe you've been working all day.'

'I certainly have,' she assured him, and gave him a radiant smile.

'Whatever you do definitely agrees with you,' he assured her as they drove off.

'I man the till on a check-out.'

His eyebrows rose. 'The supermarket kind?'

'That's right. I do other things, too,' she added. 'Help with stock, and so on.'

'I suppose it brings in some pocket money until you take off for university.'

'Some,' she said guardedly.

'Your mother will miss you when you leave home, I imagine.'

Catrin's eyes shadowed. 'Yes.'

'Your relationship is close?'

'Very close. I hate to think of her on her own. But let's change the subject or I'll start crying on your shoulder. Where are we going?'

'A place outside Tenby. I'm told the food's good,

and the hotel rather picturesque.' Ashe looked at her. 'I thought you might appreciate somewhere away from your home turf.'

It was a magical evening. The hotel was built in romantic, Gothic style, the dining room had a view of the sea, and the food was excellent. But Catrin hardly knew what she ate. She was utterly enchanted with everything, including Ashe, who was taking great pains to make everything perfect for her. He wore khakis with a pale linen jacket, just creased enough to look good, his shirt a shade of blue which did wonders for both his tan and his eyes. Catrin fell deeper and deeper in love with every passing minute, her intoxication nothing to do with the modest glass of wine that was all he would allow her.

On the way home a full moon hung in the sky like a cliché, and Catrin sat relaxed in her seat, her eyes outshining the stars. Ashe was silent for most of the journey, until he began to argue, eventually, over where they should part.

'Dammit, Cat, I can't just drop you by the roadside at this time of night,' he objected when they reached the crossroads. 'Tell me where you live.'

In the end, protest as she might, she was forced to give him directions down the last half-mile of road, telling him to pull up in the lane, out of sight of the house.

'Why so far away?' he demanded, when he'd killed the engine.

Catrin looked down at her hands. 'I—I told you to

stop here so we wouldn't be overlooked when you kiss me goodnight.'

The silence in the car was so absolute she unfastened her seat belt in an agony of embarrassment, desperate to run for home. But before she could open the car door Ashe reached for her and pulled her against him, his mouth on hers with a hot, hard urgency that made it plain he wanted this as much as she did. She melted against him, lips parted, shivering with delight as she felt his caressing tongue slide between them. Her hands wreathed around his neck to hold him closer still, but Ashe pulled away, breathing hard.

'I shouldn't be doing this,' he groaned, but she laid a finger on his lips.

'It's only a kiss,' she whispered.

Ashe rubbed his cheek against hers. 'To you, sweetheart, maybe. But if I go on kissing you I'll want more than that, so make it easy for me to let you go.'

'All right.' Catrin moved away so promptly Ashe gave a smothered curse and reached for her again, and this time they were both panting for breath when he forced himself to release her, his hands unsteady as they cupped her face. He looked down into her face, a look in his eyes which made her heart contract.

'Did I do something wrong?' she whispered.

He shook his head. 'Nothing at all. Yet. Which is why I'm sending you home to your mother right now, before I commit any real sins.'

Catrin looked at him in silence, then nodded.

'Goodnight, then, Ashe. Thank you for a perfect evening.' She smiled shyly. 'I've never been out to dinner with a man before. I'm glad you were the first.'

Ashe got out abruptly and went round the car to let her out. 'The good fortune was all on my side,' he said harshly. 'Goodnight, Cat. Will I see you tomorrow?'

She shook her head, sighing. 'Sorry. Mother runs the market garden here herself since Dad died and I help out as much as I can. And on Sunday evenings we have supper and watch television together, or go for a walk sometimes if it's fine, and she's not too tired.'

Ashe took her hand, the hard planes of his face softened in the moonlight. 'Spare some time for me next week, then.'

'If you want that.'

'You know I want it, Cat,' he said huskily. 'And if it makes you any happier I'll promise not to repeat what happened just now.'

Catrin brushed a lock of hair back from her face and looked away. 'But I've only myself to blame for that. I virtually asked you to kiss me.'

'Why, exactly?'

She hesitated. 'It just seemed like the natural end to such a magical evening.'

'Which it was, sweetheart,' he said huskily, and touched a hand to her cheek. 'I'll look forward to Monday. If this weather holds let's make an early start.'

'And if it rains?'

'I'll pick you up at eleven and you can direct me to one of those castles you were threatening me with, and this time I *will* buy you lunch.'

Catrin laughed. 'All right. But wait for me at the crossroads, please. If it's fine we'll find another beach. If not we'll do the tourist bit.'

Ashe kissed the hand he was holding and let her go. 'Goodnight, Cat. Sleep well.'

Next morning Julia Hughes woke Catrin early, looking deeply worried. 'Sorry to disturb you, darling, but I've just had a phone call from Grandma. She's had a fall and hurt her wrist. She's only shocked, and so on, but she would obviously like us to drive up there today. Hannah's on holiday in France, so we must go.'

Catrin jumped out of bed to comfort her mother, her mind working at top speed. 'Look, Mother, if it's not terribly serious with Grandma I think I'd better stay here. Beth Owen is on holiday. Three less could make things difficult.'

Julia eyed her doubtfully, but gave in with less argument than expected. 'You're right. I'd forgotten Beth. But would you mind that? With luck I should be back tonight.'

'You will not! Stay overnight, at least. It's too far to drive to Stratford and back in a day. I'll be fine.'

'I don't like to think of you on your own here at night, Catrin—'

'Mother, it's not the first time. I'm a big girl now— and we've got enough security lights and alarms to guard the crown jewels,' laughed Catrin, pulling on her clothes. 'I'll be fine. Go on, pack a bag. I'll make some breakfast.'

Despite her brave words Catrin missed her mother late that evening, when all the chores were done and everything made secure for the night. This was the one evening of the week when Julia always finished early and prepared a special meal. As soon as she was in the house Catrin rang her grandmother's number, and by the prompt way Julia answered it knew that her mother had been waiting for her call.

'Home base, here,' said Catrin cheerfully. 'All is safely gathered in, watered, or locked up, as applicable, and I'm about to make myself some supper. How's Grandma?'

To her dismay Catrin learned that her energetic grandmother was in pain, and very frustrated because her broken right wrist kept her from cooking, dressing herself and driving the car, not to mention weeding the flowerbed where the accident had happened first thing that morning.

'She tripped on the stone path, put out a hand to save herself, and bingo,' said Julia with a sigh. 'She won't admit it, but she's feeling very unwell at the moment. And Hannah's away until Thursday.'

'Then stay for a while,' urged Catrin. 'I can manage down here for a day or two. By then, knowing Grandma, she'll be expert with her left hand.'

'Are you sure, darling? I think Mother really wants me to stay, but she's too independent to ask.'

'That's settled, then. The place won't grind to a halt here without you, I promise. And Mother?'

'Yes, love?'

'Don't worry. You look after Grandma for a bit. I can look after the business.'

Which was so much the truth Julia agreed to stay in Warwickshire until her sister came back from holiday. 'But ring me every evening, the minute you're finished, and if you feel you can't manage just shout and I'll get a nurse in for Mother and come back.'

After repeated assurances Catrin put down the phone, feeling a lot less cheerful than she'd pretended to her mother. Not that she had any qualms about running the nursery. She'd been doing the accounts for her mother for some time, and the staff, most of whom had been with them for years, would rally round once they knew Julia was away. But there would be no more sunlit, beachcombing days with Ashe.

For a moment she was tempted to ring him at the hotel. But that meant she might not see him again in person at all, once he knew the situation. And she couldn't bear the thought of that. She'd take off for a few minutes next morning, and meet him at the crossroads as planned. That way she could at least talk to him, see him in the flesh. In an agony of disappointment at the thought of missing the last few days with him, Catrin gave herself a stringent lecture on priorities. Her grandmother, who was rarely ill, needed help for once, which was more important than a holiday romance no one knew about.

Catrin was proved right about the reaction from the staff. All of them professed concern for her grandmother, and assured her nothing would go wrong in Julia's absence. When she took off mid-morning to meet Ashe, Catrin told the head gardener she was going out for a few minutes, then raced up the narrow road to the meeting point, feeling dishevelled and unappealing as she opened the door of the waiting car and slid, breathless, into the passenger seat.

Ashe, casually immaculate, as usual, leaned over and kissed her flushed, damp cheek, his eyes narrowing as he took in her ancient jeans and sweatshirt. 'You're late, Cat. Something wrong?'

She nodded. 'I can't come today after all. Or any day for a while.' She explained the situation miserably, staring through the windscreen.

'You're managing that place alone?' he said incredulously.

'It's not really a case of managing—the place runs like clockwork. Most of the staff are old hands. They rallied round, just as I assured my mother they would.' Catrin stole an unhappy look at him. 'She took some persuading to stay up in Warwickshire and leave me to it, but I managed it in the end.'

'What an efficient creature you are,' he said softly, and reached out a hand to brush back a lock of hair from her disconsolate face. 'So what do I do with myself now, Catrin?'

'Lie on the beach somewhere, if I were you.' Catrin eyed the sky suspiciously. 'Something tells me the weather's going to break.'

'I suppose I should be grateful it's been kind so long.' He took her hand in his, playing with her fingers. 'I appreciate that you don't have time for me in the day, Cat, but what about the evenings? Let me take you out tonight.'

Catrin was sorely tempted, but in the end she shook her head ruefully. 'I can't tonight, Ashe. I won't finish until late. Then I've got to do the books. And by that time I'll probably be very poor company.'

Ashe's grip tightened. 'In that case give me your phone number. I need to ring you, at least, to make sure you're all in one piece at the end of the day.'

She watched him scribble the number on a card from his wallet, then said goodbye. 'I must go. Sorry, Ashe.'

'Not as sorry as I am,' he assured her, and leaned over to kiss her mouth. 'Don't work too hard. I'll talk to you tonight.'

Catrin nodded, close to tears, and slid out of the car, giving him a brief wave before she hurried away to make good her promise to keep everything working smoothly until her mother got back.

During the afternoon the clouds began to roll in from the sea, and by the time Catrin finished for the day the rain was coming down in sheets. She did a double-check on everything, then went in the house to ring her mother, ask about her grandmother, and report on the day. Then she had a hot shower before getting to grips with the accounts for an hour. Afterwards, she promised herself, she would cook herself something easy and eat her supper while she finished the thriller she'd been taking to the beach for days.

Catrin finished her meal, washed up, and with a sigh of relief settled on a sofa in the sitting room with her book just as the storm, which had been rumbling round all evening, broke in earnest. Loud crashes of thunder were almost simultaneous with lightning flashes that filled up the entire sky, and Catrin prowled through the upstairs rooms, enjoying the display, but praying there would be no hail to create havoc with the unprotected crops.

After a while the storm grew less fierce, and, relieved, she went downstairs, stopping halfway in alarm at the sound of hammering on the seldom-used front door. Then she heard Ashe calling her name, and flew down the remaining stairs to open the door, her eyes wide with astonishment.

'Good heavens, what are *you* doing here?'

'I was worried. Are you all right, sweetheart?' he asked urgently.

Catrin undid the safety-chain to let him in, smiling at him radiantly. 'Yes, fine. I was a bit worried for a while—'

'Afraid of thunder?'

'Hail, not thunder. It can do a lot of damage. But it didn't happen tonight, thank goodness. Good grief, just look at you. You're soaked through.' Catrin eyed his wet shirt and thin cotton trousers with concern. 'Go up to the bathroom. First on the right at the top of the stairs. Take those wet things off, and I'll dry them. There's a blue towelling robe behind the door. How on earth did you get so wet?'

Ashe pushed back his streaming hair, his smile

wry. 'I parked the car the requisite distance from the house.'

'I thought you were going to ring me,' she said, secretly delirious with delight at the sight of him.

'I was. But I hated the thought of you alone in this place in a storm. I had visions of power failure, you feeling terrified. So, much as I wrestled with myself, in the end I had to come.' He shook his head. 'But I needn't have worried. You're obviously well in control. My knight-errantry wasn't necessary, after all.'

'I'm delighted to see you, whatever your reason for coming.' Catrin assured him. 'But please go upstairs and change. Have you had dinner?'

'Yes. Have you?'

'Yes. But I'll make us some coffee. If you like,' she added, then flushed at the look in his eyes.

'I like very much,' said Ashe huskily.

While he was upstairs Catrin flew round the kitchen, making coffee, taking a fruitcake out of tin, and when Ashe came in with a bundle of wet clothes she thrust them in the dryer, grinning at the sight of him in her mother's navy blue robe.

'I trust this is the garment you meant,' he said, laughing. 'The only other one available was a very short, yellow affair.'

'Mine,' Catrin told him, her eyes dancing.

'At least this one's respectable, as long as I don't move about too much!' He grinned. 'Where do you want me to take this tray?'

'Back along the hall. Our little den looks out on

the nurseries. Mother likes to keep an eye on her domain at all times.'

'She sounds like quite a lady,' commented Ashe, as he followed Catrin into a small, welcoming room. 'This is charming.' He put the tray down on a small table, and raised a questioning eyebrow. 'Would she object to my presence here tonight?'

Catrin filled cups, frowning. 'In the circumstances, I don't *think* she would. Fancy a slice of cake? One of the older women brought it in for me today, convinced I'll starve while Mother's away.'

'I'd like some coffee but I'll pass on the cake.' Ashe took the cup she offered, and sat down beside her on the sofa. 'I wondered if you'd gone to bed already, worn out by your day.'

'There were accounts to do after I locked up, then I had a shower, and made myself some supper, by which time the storm was in full swing—' She halted at the look in his eyes. 'What is it?'

'Catrin,' he said abruptly. 'I was lying.'

She bit her lip. 'About what?'

'About the storm. I intended coming tonight anyway.'

She bowed her head, her hair falling forward to hide her face. 'Because my mother's not here?'

'No. Because I damn well couldn't keep away.' Ashe caught her by the chin, bringing her face round, his spectacular eyes glittering in the dark tan of his face. 'I knew you were alone tonight. I argued with myself, told myself to be sensible. But I lost the argument long before the storm gave me the excuse to come.'

Catrin stared at him dumbly, her heart hammering, with no idea how to reply. In the end it seemed best to be honest. 'I'm not much good at subterfuge,' she said gruffly. 'You must know I'm glad you came. It was so hard this morning to tell you I couldn't see you again. Which is idiotic. You're leaving soon, anyway.'

'I know,' he said unevenly. 'But not yet, sweetheart, not yet.'

They looked at each other for a long, tense moment, then Catrin gave him a shaky smile, and Ashe let out a deep breath and drew her onto his lap, smoothing the head she laid against his shoulder.

For a brief, blissful interval it was enough to lie quiet in Ashe's embrace, but the temptation to touch him was too great, and at last Catrin slid a hand under the towelling robe to smooth the warm, tanned skin of his chest, as she'd so often longed to do. She raised her head to smile at him in sleepy invitation, and his eyes darkened in the instant before he bent his head to kiss her fiercely. His hungry mouth and seeking tongue banished the dreamy contentment of before, his caressing hands arousing hot, shivering sensations Catrin had never known existed. She was astonished as her entire body caught fire, ignited to a fever-pitch of molten longing for something she knew, beyond all doubt, only Ashe could give her.

With shaking hands, his eyes asking a question she answered without words, he stripped her shirt off and slid the jeans from her slender, unresisting hips, then stopped dead, his eyes closed and hands clenched.

'What is it?' she gasped.

'I can't—I don't have—'

'I take the necessary pills,' she assured him gruffly, and got to her feet to strip off the last scraps of underwear. He was breathing hard, his eyes dark now with the need he was fighting to keep under control. He stripped off the robe and drew her down to lie beside him, his hands moulding her against him, and a jolt like an electric shock ran through her as her bare skin came in contact with his flesh which told her, more eloquently than any words, how much he wanted to bury himself inside her and assuage the burning hunger overwhelming them both.

But even as Ashe kissed her Catrin knew he was keeping an iron control over himself as his lips and fingers caressed and aroused every eager part of her into such melting response that when he finally surrendered to her smothered pleas the small, inevitable pain she felt went almost unnoticed in the accompanying joy of relief. He raised his head sharply, his eyes dark with shock for a moment, then she moved against him and he responded involuntarily, his body quickly initiating hers into a rhythm which he fought to keep slow and gentle at first, but which soon progressed to a mounting, thrusting rapture which, all too soon, drowned her in a flood of sensation so new and astonishing she uttered a cry of pure triumph and clutched Ashe close in her arms until he gasped in the throes of his own release, his heart hammering against hers.

Ashe raised his head and looked into her eyes, which glittered in the subdued lamplight.

'Now I know,' he said huskily.

'Know what?'

'What colour your eyes are when you're naked.'

CHAPTER FIVE

CATRIN stretched, and gave him a lazy little smile. 'What colour are they, then?'

'Glittery and gold, like a beautiful little tiger cat,' he said softly, smoothing the damp hair back from her face.

'Yours,' she informed him, 'go black. The dark rims round the blue bits expand and blend into the pupils.'

'Do they?' he said, astonished.

'Hasn't anyone ever told you that before?'

'No.' Ashe's eyelids came down like shutters, and Catrin touched a hand to his cheek in dismay.

'Was I supposed to keep mine closed? Sorry. I don't know the rules. But I didn't want to miss anything. And, though it's obvious it was the first time for me, don't try and tell me it was for you.'

Ashe stared down at her bleakly. 'I won't, because it's not. Hell, Catrin, I've got a good few years' start on you.' He raised an expressive eyebrow. 'You gave me quite a surprise, sweetheart. After your mention of pills I didn't expect you to be—'

'A virgin,' said Catrin bluntly. 'The pills are Mother's idea, a sensible precaution in case of accidents, particularly as I'm going away to college. But until now they've never been necessary.' She eyed him curiously. 'I thought if I told you it was my first time you'd stop. And, as perhaps you noticed, I didn't want you to. Should I have warned you? How do you feel about it?'

'Like Columbus discovering America!' He looked deep into her eyes. 'And you, sweetheart? Was it what you'd imagined?'

'How could I possibly have imagined anything like—like *that*?' She smiled mischievously. 'Friends have insisted on giving me a blow-by-blow description of their first time at this kind of thing, but the overall impression I got from everyone was that it was no big deal!'

Ashe pulled her to her feet and held her close. 'Is that how *you* feel?'

'No. I just feel very sorry for them,' said Catrin, looking up into his eyes. 'Nor, in case you're wondering, will I ever talk about it. I don't want to share it with anyone. Pointless, anyway. No one would ever believe me, Ashe.'

He bent to kiss her. 'I'd like to say I tried my best to make it beautiful for you, and at first I did try. But in the end what happened between us just—happened.'

'Then I'm lucky,' she said, touching a hand to his cheek.

Ashe shook his head. 'I'm the lucky one, sweetheart.' He sighed deeply, and released her. 'I must go, and let you get to bed.'

'Some of us worker bees have to be up in the morning,' she agreed regretfully, and pulled on her jeans and shirt, her shyness a thing of the past. 'I'll get your things from the dryer. It might cause comment if you creep into the hotel wearing my mother's dressing gown.'

Ashe laughed, and followed her to the kitchen to pull on the creased, half-dried clothes she handed him. 'So. Will you be too tired to let me take you out to dinner tomorrow night?'

'I thought,' she said, studying her fingernails, 'that you might like to come and have supper with me here.'

Ashe pulled her into his arms and kissed her. 'You thought right, sweetheart. But no way am I going to let you slave over a meal after a day's work. I'll bring something.'

Catrin thought for a moment. 'If you fancy a trip into Haverfordwest tomorrow you could pick up some ham, or whatever, to go with my own spanking fresh salad vegetables, then any cooking will be minimal.'

'Done!' he said promptly, then eyed her challengingly. 'Am I required to wear a disguise, and creep along the road at dusk?'

She laughed. 'No, I suppose not. Just give me time to do my chores and so on, then I'm yours—' She stopped dead, blushed to the roots of her hair, and Ashe caught her in his arms and held her cruelly tight.

'Sweetheart, I wish I didn't have to go,' he murmured against her mouth. 'It's going to be a long, boring day tomorrow. How early can I come to dinner?'

* * *

Julia Hughes rang next evening, to ask if Catrin could manage until Saturday, when help was at hand for her grandmother. Hannah, Julia's sister, was taking extra time from her high-powered job, but would need a day's grace after her arrival from France before going to Stratford.

'Of course, I can,' said Catrin, with such enthusiasm her mother thanked her lovingly, fired off several questions about the business and the staff, instructed her daughter to eat well and get to bed early, and rang off, obviously reassured.

Julia Hughes would not, Catrin knew, have been so happy had she known exactly how her daughter was spending her time. Catrin consoled herself that she worked hard during the day and never neglected any of the necessary chores after the nursery was closed, though she took to completing them at top speed, to allow time to make herself as attractive as possible for Ashe. The first evening they made a pretence of watching television after the simple meal, but before long Catrin was in Ashe's arms, where she'd longed to be all day.

'Sweetheart,' he said hoarsely against her lips. 'I haven't come just for this. Though Lord knows it's all I've been thinking of since last night.'

'So have I,' she said with candour, and smiled into the darkening blue eyes. 'Last night you said you wanted to go to bed with me. Let's do that now.'

'Cat,' he said in desperation. 'We shouldn't. *I* shouldn't—'

'Why not?' she demanded. 'Normally I'm never

alone in the house. So why refuse something fate's arranged so neatly for us? Unless,' she added, drawing away, 'I disappointed you last night, of course. Perhaps I wasn't—'

Ashe stopped her mouth with his, telling her without words that far from being disappointed in her he wanted her so badly that in minutes his scruples were banished, and they were together in the double bed she'd slept in all her life. And this time the loving was less precipitate. Ashe took slow, tantalising delight in discovering exactly what gave her maximum pleasure, afterwards teaching her how to please him in return. Catrin forgot any last shreds of reserve in the newness and wonder of it all, and it was long after midnight when Ashe tore himself away. And afterwards Catrin lay wakeful, reliving every minute of this new, addictive rapture before she surrendered to sleep.

Successive days of getting up early after sleeping very little, of working hard all day afterwards, would have given Catrin's eyes shadows without the evenings of lovemaking, which grew more feverish and intense as the days went by. Julia was due home on Saturday, Ashe would be leaving on Sunday, and after that the idyll would be over.

When Ashe made a move to leave her, late on the Friday night, he took Catrin's face into his hands and looked deep into her heavy eyes. 'Tomorrow night I've booked dinner at the place near Tenby again. What time will you be free?'

'About eight? I'll come to the crossroads,' she whispered, leaning tiredly against him.

He smiled crookedly, smoothing her tumbled hair back. 'Clandestine to the last. But tomorrow night, sweetheart, we'll sort out a few things over dinner.'

'What sort of things?'

'Necessary evils,' he said lightly, his tone at odds with the bleak look in his eyes. He kissed her quickly, then kissed her again with sudden, renewed hunger. Catrin's curiosity left her, replaced by the now familiar mounting excitement, and she made no protest, urgent as Ashe when he picked her up and took her back to bed again. This time they fell asleep afterwards in each other's arms, and the sky was already beginning to pale when Ashe woke with a start, gave Catrin a swift, apologetic kiss, and leapt out of bed to pull on his clothes and race downstairs to let himself out.

In consequence Catrin was looking less than her best when Julia arrived home that afternoon, and came out to find her daughter in one of the hothouses.

'Goodness, Catrin, just look at you,' she said in concern, kissing her.

'Take her away and make her have a rest,' said Bryn Thomas, the head gardener. 'Everything's fine; not a thing went wrong. Catrin's been working her socks off, Mrs Hughes. Good as gold, she's been.'

Not entirely, thought Catrin guiltily, and asked after her grandmother, and Hannah, who was a great favourite with her niece.

'I've been fine,' Catrin assured her mother as they went back to the house.

'Not too lonely?'

'No.' Catrin hesitated for a moment, then said with a rush, 'Actually, the boy I met—remember? His name's Ashe, and he came round for an hour in the evenings to keep me company. I hope you don't mind. But he's going back tomorrow, and otherwise I wouldn't have managed to see him. I was too done in to go out by the time I'd finished work—' And I'm babbling like an idiot, she thought as she came to a halt.

'Of course I don't mind,' said Julia absently, tidying stray locks back into the hair that was coiled up less neatly than usual. 'My car broke down while I was there, by the way, and I've had to leave it at a garage to wait for some expensive part.'

'So how did you get home?' asked Catrin. 'You look very hot—I hope you didn't have to walk!' She bent to unload the washing machine, missing the tide of colour which rose in her mother's face.

'A friend—of Grandma's, I mean—was coming down this way to visit friends this weekend. I—I was able to beg a lift,' said Julia rather breathlessly, and eyed the bedlinen Catrin was folding into a basket. 'You needn't have done laundry as well, darling!'

Catrin shrugged, smiling. 'Washed, but not ironed. I'm going out tonight, by the way,' she added casually. 'I hope you don't mind.'

'Of course not.' Julia smiled teasingly. 'The mysterious young Ashe again?'

'That's right. I won't be late.'

* * *

Julia insisted on taking on the evening chores herself, and sent her daughter off for a rest and a bath to prepare for her evening. Catrin took a long time over her hair, her eyes dreamy as she brushed it into a glossy frame for her narrow, tanned face. Tonight her eyes were green, courtesy of the filmy lawn dress, and for once she used eyeshadow to emphasise it, and mascara on her lashes. Tonight Ashe had things to discuss with her, he'd said, and Catrin sat at her window, looking down onto the private little garden, wondering what he had in mind. Surely he wouldn't just say goodbye and go on his way. Not after the heavenly time they'd spent together this week.

Catrin said goodbye to her mother and walked slowly to the crossroads, so sure Ashe's car would be waiting there she stared blankly when it was nowhere in sight. She leaned against the old stone wall in the sunset light, her eyes fixed on the road, but though cars passed from time to time, raising her hopes, none of them belonged to Ashe.

Half an hour passed, during which Catrin thought of a hundred possible reasons why Ashe was late. Waiting like this was new in their relationship. Ashe had always been before her up to now. Perhaps he'd had an accident. Or he was ill. But he had her phone number. He could have rung, perhaps he had after she left home! Her eyes brightening, Catrin hurried home, and burst into the small sitting room.

'What's the matter?' demanded Julia in alarm.

'Has anyone phoned?' panted Catrin.

'No, darling. No one.'

'Have *you* been on the phone, then?'

Julia shook her head, frowning. 'I assume Ashe didn't turn up.'

'No, he didn't. There must be something wrong.' Catrin raced from the room. In the hall she rang the Sea View Hotel, and asked for Dr Ashe.

'Who, Catrin?' answered Mrs Marshall coolly.

Catrin ground her teeth in frustration. Mrs Marshall knew perfectly well who she meant. 'Dr Ashe—the man you saw me with on the beach.'

'Ah, yes,' said Mrs Marshall, her voice heavy with disapproval. 'I'm afraid the gentleman left this afternoon.'

'Left?' said Catrin blankly.

'That's right. He was booked until tomorrow, but he paid his bill this afternoon in rather a hurry. Called away, he said.'

'Did he leave any messages?'

'None, I'm afraid.' There was a pause, then Mrs Marshall, who'd known Catrin since she was born, went on rather more gently, 'I think you should know, Catrin, that his name was actually Ellison, and, although he came alone, the original booking was made for him *and* his wife.'

Catrin stood turned to stone. 'I see,' she said numbly at last. 'So sorry to trouble you, Mrs Marshall. Goodbye.'

Catrin put the phone down with a trembling hand, feeling ill with shock. She went into the small cloakroom off the hall and stared at her face in the mirror. How odd. She looked just the same. She waited for a few minutes to pull herself together, then squared her shoulders and went back to her mother. 'He's gone. Called away.' She smiled brightly. 'He left a message to say he couldn't make it, but he'd see me next time he was down.'

'What a shame.' Julia got up briskly. 'But if you're not going out you need something to eat. You've lost weight since I saw you last, my girl.'

Since Julia Hughes believed Ashe was just one of the holidaymakers who came in their thousands to the area every summer, Catrin was obliged to put on the performance of her life to hide her shock at Mrs Marshall's revelation. At first it was impossible to take in the fact that Ashe had given her a false name, let alone assimilate the bitter, unbelievable news that he was married. Then anger succeeded the original shock. Dr Ellison, as she must remember to think of him, had obviously needed diversion on his holiday, and she burned with shame and rage at her naive willingness to provide it—even inviting him into the same bed where she now spent long, sleepless nights willing herself to forget him. And his lovemaking.

The weather was good for most of that summer, but Catrin went no more to the beach. Instead she threw herself into a hectic social life with any school-friends available. And during the day she worked as hard as she could at the market garden, doing her best to lighten her mother's load in any way possible, now she knew what it was like to shoulder the responsibility alone. Novelty was supplied by a visit from her grandmother and Aunt Hannah, so that there were four of them to celebrate when Catrin's results came through, confirming her place at university.

One way and another, thought Catrin bitterly, girlhood was over. It was time to get on with the rest of her life.

CHAPTER SIX

AFTER telling Dinah the somewhat edited version of her story Catrin found she felt surprisingly better. Sharing her secret at last had been good for her, and in some strange way accelerated her recovery. By the time her mother returned from Zermatt the following weekend Catrin could truthfully say she felt fine. Julia had already heard about the fire from Liam, but Catrin was able to assure her horrified mother that she'd suffered no ill effects, she was back in work and life was normal again.

Catrin asked about the holiday, promised to spend the weekend of Liam's half-term in Stratford, then settled down to enjoy the rest of her lazy Sunday evening in front of the fire with a book. Her sitting room felt cosy and peaceful with the lamps lit, brick-red linen curtains shutting out the February sleet, and when her doorbell rang later she frowned impatiently, hoping it wasn't Julian. Her first week back at the office had been hectic. She didn't feel like company. With an impatient sigh Catrin crossed to the door and picked up the receiver, then almost dropped it.

'Ashe,' said the last voice she'd expected to hear. 'Spare me a few minutes, please, Catrin.'

She stood still, tempted to tell him to go away, that he'd interrupted a passionate session with an imaginary lover. Then curiosity got the better of her and she pressed the button to release the main door.

In the short time it took her visitor to mount the stairs Catrin added a few touches to her face, and had herself well in hand when she opened her door to Ashe.

He stood just inside the room for a moment, looking different both from the Ashe of long ago, and from the elegant-suited consultant of more recent acquaintance. He wore a rain-soaked suede jacket over moleskins and a heavy sweater, his hair was wet, and, to Catrin's irritation, his dishevelment only added to his appeal. His unexpected physical presence on her own territory set her senses adrift, rousing an unwanted leap of response inside her.

'I hope I don't intrude,' he said formally.

'Not at all,' she replied in kind, pulling herself together. 'I was just reading.'

'I've tried ringing, as you know, but with no success,' he went on, 'otherwise I would have made an appointment—'

'You're the consultant, not me. I don't make appointments.' She waved him to a chair. 'Shall I take your jacket? It looks wet.'

'Thank you.' He handed it over, then waited for her to return to the sofa before sitting down. 'How are you feeling?'

'Perfectly well now. I returned to work a week ago,' she said calmly. 'Once the stitches were gone I improved rapidly—in health if not in looks. Though I'm told the scar will fade.'

'It's not noticeable under your hair.'

'Why are you here?' she asked bluntly. 'I didn't think consultants made house-calls.'

He held up a hand like a fencer, acknowledging the hit. 'I'm not here in a professional capacity.'

'I never thought for a moment that you were!'

Ashe looked at her in silence, as though trying to rediscover the young Catrin in the composed young woman who sat looking at him like a judge passing sentence. She wore black corded velvet trousers and a silver-grey sweater, the latter, as Catrin knew very well, rendering her eyes as clear as glass. And equally cold.

'Why didn't you return my calls, Catrin?' he asked at last.

'Why did you want me to?' she countered.

'You know why,' he said huskily, sitting forward in the chair. 'Fate has thrown us together again, Catrin, and I, at least, am grateful to it. From the moment I saw you in that hospital bed I haven't stopped thinking about you. And don't try to lie. You're no more indifferent to me than I am to you.'

She smiled derisively. 'Still confident of your own charm, I see. But in no position to talk about lies!'

His eyes narrowed. 'What do you mean?'

'If you don't know, there's not much point in discussing it. Besides, none of it really matters any more.'

Ashe sat looking at her in silence, eyeing her thoughtfully. 'I don't believe that,' he said at last.

'But if you won't talk about us, Catrin, let's talk about Liam instead.'

Catrin stared at him, frustrated. 'I don't understand. Why this extraordinary preoccupation with my brother, Ashe?'

'Surely that's obvious,' he retorted.

'Not to me!'

Ashe rose restlessly and went to stand staring down into the flickering gas-fired logs set into the fireplace. 'Can't we stop fencing, Catrin?'

'If I knew what you were talking about I'd be happy to,' she informed him tartly. 'What's so fascinating to you about my brother? He's just an ordinary nine-year-old—'

'But he's not, is he?' pounced Ashe, turning on her. 'Admit it. He's my son.'

'*What?*' Catrin shook her head vehemently. 'He certainly is not your son. He's my half-brother. My mother married again not long after—after I last saw you. Liam was born the following year.'

His eyes narrowed. 'But I always assumed she was in her sixties, like your father. Would you mind telling me how old your mother actually is?'

'Not in the least. She's forty-seven. Thirty-eight when Liam was born.' Catrin got up. 'So now we've cleared that little point up perhaps you'd go.'

'Not yet.' Ashe's eyes speared hers. 'I still think it's a coincidence that ten years after our brief idyll I find you in possession of a brother of the right age who just happens to have blue eyes and black hair like mine.'

'I'm afraid that's exactly what it is,' she retorted. 'Coincidence, pure and simple. Liam was nine on Christmas Eve. You're not an obstetrician, but I'm sure you can work that one out. Our little *idyll*,' she said with scorn, 'took place in August, so the statistics are a bit out for your theory.'

'Statistics can be forged,' he said, unmoved. 'Your relationship with your mother was very close. I'm sure she would have agreed to bring the baby up as her own.'

'Liam *is* her own,' said Catrin emphatically. 'Your story is pure fiction. Why are you so keen on claiming him as your son, Dr Hope-Ellison? Are your children girls? No son to carry on your double-barrelled name?'

'I don't have any children. Nor,' he added without expression, 'do I have a wife.'

'You did once,' she said, very quietly.

For a long, tense interval the flickering of the artificial flames was the only sound in the room.

'So you found out,' he said at last, his face suddenly haggard. 'How?'

'When you stood me up that night I rang the hotel. I was told that you'd left in a hurry, and your *wife* had originally been booked to share your room. I assumed you were hurrying back to her.' Catrin's eyes were like discs of ice. 'Mrs Marshall said your name was Ellison, too, which rather threw me. She seemed to have lost the Hope bit. I lost hope too, after that. A false name *and* a wife were altogether too much to swallow.' She turned on her heel and went to the kitchen, annoyed to find she was shaking with anger. She took a moment or two to recover her self-control, and when she rejoined Ashe she was composed again as she handed him his jacket. 'Goodbye.'

He took the garment from her and tossed it on the floor. 'No, Catrin. You can't hurl all that at me and expect me to go away without giving you my side of the story.'

'"Story" being the operative word,' she said stonily. 'I've listened to your nonsense about Liam, but I'm bored now. I don't want to hear any more.'

'Which is unfortunate,' he said, equally cold, and grasped her wrists. 'Because I want you to listen.'

Catrin tensed, utterly mortified to feel a rush of unwanted reaction to his touch. 'Let me go,' she snapped.

Ashe released her and stepped back. 'I apologise,' he said stiffly. 'But I insist on your listening to the truth.'

'Truth!' she mocked. 'Not something you practised back then when I was young, Dr Hope-Ellison.'

'I'm just Ashe, Catrin,' he said quietly. 'Just as I was then.' He breathed in deeply. 'For several reasons my time with you was like a healing process for me. I liked pretending that I was just Ashe. He was a lucky swine with nothing to stop him having a relationship with a girl like you. But I knew you deserved the truth before I left. That Saturday night I was going to tell you everything—my full name, all about my wife. I was going to ask you to wait for me until I sorted my life out.'

Catrin sat down suddenly on the sofa. 'So why didn't you?' she asked dully.

'I went walking that afternoon, to kill time, and ended up wandering past your place like a lovesick schoolboy. About half a mile away there was a lane.' Ashe sat down again in the chair, his eyes absent, as though he were looking inward at a picture in his mind. 'I assumed it was a short cut back to the main road so I went along there, suddenly impatient to get back to the hotel and get ready for the evening with you.' He gave her a challenging look. 'From here on I imagine you know what I'm going to say.'

Catrin shook her head, mystified. 'Afraid not.'

'You know the lane I mean?'

'Of course I do. It bordered our property.'

'Then cast your mind back. A mile or so along it there was an entrance into a field. I saw a car parked there, half-hidden under the trees. Are you with me?' he demanded.

'No. Should I be?' she said blankly.

'In the car,' he went on, 'there were two people, oblivious to everything in the world. They were locked in each other's arms, kissing as though they couldn't get enough of each other.' Ashe looked her in the eye.

'Wait a minute! Are you saying you thought the girl was *me*?' said Catrin incredulously.

'I *know* it was you,' he said with emphasis.

There was a taut, simmering silence in the room for a moment or two, then Catrin said flatly, 'You were mistaken.'

'I suppose you were bound to say that.' He shrugged. 'It doesn't matter a damn now, anyway. It's a long time ago. I'm only telling you so you'll know why I turned tail and ran that day. After my experience with my wife you had been like a breath of fresh air to me, untouched and totally guileless. Then I found virginal little Catrin in another man's arms, his hands all over her.' Ashe paused, his jaw clenched. 'After what had happened between us the night before I just couldn't take it. I went berserk, ready to commit murder, so I ran like hell, before I could do any damage.'

Catrin stared at him blankly. 'I can't believe this. First you assume Liam is your son—which is pretty big of you, considering I was supposed to be messing around with someone else.'

'The whole reason for thinking Liam is my son is that he looks like me. It's impossible that anyone else could have fathered him,' said Ashe, with conviction.

Shaken to the core, Catrin looked at him in silence for some time. 'Liam is neither my son nor yours, Ashe,' she said at last. 'And it wasn't me you saw in that car, either. I was working hard all day to make the time pass until I saw you again that night. If you'd only come and confronted me with it I could have produced several witnesses to corroborate my story. Instead,' she added bitterly, 'you bolted, and broke my stupid little heart in the process.'

Ashe got up and pulled her to her feet, staring down into her eyes. 'Are you telling me the truth?' he demanded.

'Yes, I am! Not that I care whether you believe me or not,' she informed him angrily, and stared down at his restraining hands until he removed them. 'As you said, it's a long time ago. I hadn't thought of you in years until I landed myself in Pennington General.'

'I tried to get in touch afterwards, back then,' he said abruptly.

Catrin stilled. 'When?'

'A few months later.' He shrugged. 'All that time, no matter how much I tried, I couldn't get you out of my mind. I got over my wife a hell of a sight better than I got over you. And in the end I was prepared to forgive you for the episode in the car—'

'How very magnanimous of you,' said Catrin, eyes glittering. 'Read my lips, Ashe. It wasn't me.'

'So you say.' He looked away. 'Anyway, I finally gave in and rang your house. But the business was under new management.'

Catrin nodded. 'Our head gardener formed a co-operative with some of the other employees and bought the market garden from Mother. And soon afterwards she got married again.'

'Were you happy about that?'

'Yes. I like my stepfather very much.'

Ashe looked down at her, a wry twist to his mouth. 'The man I contacted at your place flatly refused to provide a stranger with any information about you. So I rang the Sea View Hotel, but by that time the Marshalls had retired, and the new people were strangers to the district. I was foiled at every turn. I never asked you which university you were heading for, so I couldn't even trace you that way, either. In the end I decided it was time to stop behaving like an idiot over a holiday fling, and put you out of my mind for good.'

There was a long silence, filled on Catrin's part with bittersweet regret for what might have been. What Ashe was thinking about she had no idea. His contained face betrayed nothing.

Eventually he bent to pick up his jacket, and for a moment Catrin considered offering him tea, or a drink, then decided against it. What was the point? This man was a stranger. 'I'm sorry your time's been wasted,' she said politely.

'I don't look on time spent in your company as a waste, Catrin.' He smiled, and for an instant he was no longer a stranger but the Ashe of old.

Catrin, taken off guard for an instant, went to the door quickly, giving Ashe no choice but to follow. She held out her hand formally and he took it, but instead of shaking it briefly and releasing it, as she'd expected, he held it in a light, impersonal grasp, looking down at her very gravely.

'*Are* you telling me the truth, Catrin? About Liam?'

She sighed impatiently. 'So we're back to that again. Yes, I am telling the truth. He is not your son. I love him to bits, but he's not *my* son, either; he's my kid brother.' She paused, frowning. 'Why, Ashe? If he were mine—and yours—what did you mean to do about it?'

Ashe released her hand. 'Make you admit it, for a start. Which you're obviously unwilling to do.'

'Unwilling!' She moved away, folding her arms across her chest. 'How can I admit to something which isn't true?'

'I have only your word for that,' he pointed out.

Catrin eyed him coldly. 'If I thought we were likely to meet again I would give you full confirmation of Liam's birth and his parentage. But we're not. Liam is nothing to do with you. If you want a son, get one in the usual way. I assume you found another wife?' she added, as an afterthought.

'No. One marriage was enough. I prefer less binding relationships these days.' Ashe looked down at her ringless hand. 'You're not married, either.'

'No, I'm not,' she said curtly.

His eyes moved over her in a thoughtful, impersonal way. 'Obviously through preference. You've matured into a very attractive lady. A little more rounded than the girl I knew, but that, as I'm sure you're well aware, merely adds to the appeal.'

To her intense irritation Catrin couldn't come up with a witty, scathing retort. Instead she opened the door. 'Goodbye, Ashe. I'm sorry it was a wasted trip for you, but at least I now know why I was left waiting at the crossroads that night.' She frowned. 'But if you were so disgusted and angry about the girl in the car—my double, apparently—you should have just met me as planned and given me hell about it.'

Ashe thought for a moment, his eyes absent. 'I think I would have,' he said slowly, 'if I could have confronted you right away. I remember wanting to wrench that car door open and at the very least give you a good hiding.'

She laughed scornfully. 'You'd have given some poor girl a shock if you had—not to mention risking grievous bodily harm from the lover!'

'I'm glad you find it so hilarious.' His face set in grim lines. 'Until recently it's a hell of a long time since I've given that day a thought. But meeting you seems to have brought it into focus. Looking back, I can clearly remember rage and sick, blinding jealousy, then the overpowering desire to run. To put as much distance between that car and myself as possible. By the time I reached the hotel I'd persuaded myself I never wanted to set eyes on you again, so I checked out and drove to Scotland.'

'All the way to Scotland in a rage?' she said, shaking her head. 'Goodness. A wonder you didn't kill yourself—or someone else. Why Scotland?'

'My parents lived there at the time. I merely arrived a bit earlier than expected. I spent a day or two with them, as promised, then went off to Birmingham to my new job.' Ashe went outside onto the landing, looking down at her. 'Thank you for talking to me, Catrin.'

'Not at all.' She smiled politely. 'Goodbye, Ashe.'

'Does it have to be goodbye?'

'Perhaps we'll bump into each other now and then,' she said noncommittally. 'Pennington's a smallish town—' She broke off as the buzzer sounded on her intercom. 'Excuse me.' She listened to the voice on the other end, and with a little sigh said, 'Julian.

Hello. Yes, of course. Come up.' Catrin replaced the receiver, smiling wryly. 'My day for visitors.'

'Your lover?' enquired Ashe lightly.

She shrugged noncommittally, telling him without words that it was none of his business. 'Goodnight.'

'Goodnight, Catrin.' He smiled into her eyes in a way Julian Fellowes very obviously took exception to as he came up the stairs to join them.

Catrin was forced to make introductions and take leave of Ashe under the somewhat affronted gaze of Julian, who obviously hadn't expected to find Catrin entertaining another man. He told her so in no uncertain terms when Ashe had gone.

'Why?' said Catrin.

'Why what?' said Julian blankly.

'Why was it a surprise to find another man here? I do have other friends, Julian.'

'I thought I was rather more than just a friend,' he said stiffly, and Catrin laughed and offered him a drink.

'No, you didn't, Julian. You like things the way they are, just as I do. A friendly evening together now and then with no strings and no recriminations on either side when the arrangement breaks down occasionally. As it tends to do.'

A swallow or two of whisky mellowed Julian enough to stop feeling offended, and, after asking if she were fully recovered, and coping with her working life again, he reverted to the subject of Ashe. 'Who is this Hope-Ellison chap, anyway?'

'Someone I knew years ago when I lived in Wales.'

Catrin explained how she'd met Ashe again at the hospital, then changed the subject with finality.

It was only later, when she had arranged to meet Julian another night and sent him on his way, that Catrin had the opportunity to mull over the visit from Ashe. It was a long time since she'd let herself wonder why he'd vanished so abruptly that summer. Now she knew. And his explanation was pretty far-fetched. Probably pure fiction, too. The more likely explanation, she decided cynically, was a sudden backing off in case little Cat had harboured expectations.

It was the other surprise he'd sprung on her which made her more uneasy. No wonder he'd been interested in Liam at the hospital. Nor did she blame Ashe for taking to the boy. Liam was a bright, attractive lad, irritating, noisy and downright naughty at times, like all his kind, but affectionate and miraculously unspoilt, despite the headcount of doting female relatives. But Ashe couldn't have him. Not, Catrin reminded herself, that he'd said what he actually wanted. But something in Ashe's manner was disquieting when he spoke of Liam.

She felt uneasier still when Ashe rang later.

'I hope I'm not disturbing you, Catrin. Do you go early to bed?' he asked, his tone making it clear that if she was in bed with Julian he was only too glad to have disturbed her.

'It all depends,' she said evenly, 'on what you mean by early. During my working week I try to get to bed before midnight.'

'Very sensible.' He paused. 'I'm ringing because

we were interrupted earlier. I was about to suggest dinner some evening.'

'I don't think that's a good idea, Ashe.'

'No ulterior motive, I promise.'

'I might as well be honest,' she said bluntly. 'If I thought my company was your only motive I might well say yes. But I think you've still got a bee in your bonnet about Liam—'

'No,' he contradicted quickly. 'I admit I put two and two together and got five, and I want to atone for my mistake. Past *and* present,' he added.

For a moment Catrin was tempted. But seeing him again had revived old hurts she had believed were long since healed. And because he still possessed the hint of danger that had always been part of his charm she shook her head, unseen. 'I don't think so, Ashe,' she said at last. 'I really don't know you any more. Not, of course, that I ever really did.' She put the phone down gently, and feeling suddenly exhausted, she took herself off to bed.

CHAPTER SEVEN

FOR a day or two Catrin half expected to hear from Ashe again, but there were no more phone calls, nor messages left on her machine, and after a week spent in the way she'd been accustomed to before the fire—a dinner with Julian, trips to the cinema and the theatre with Dinah, or friends from the office—she felt that life was, at last, returning to something like its usual routine. And if the word 'routine' conjured up a boring picture, Catrin welcomed it. Better a safe, uncomplicated lifestyle than the dangerous tension which Ashe Hope-Ellison still generated whenever he was in her vicinity. She was no longer in love with him. She wasn't sure she even liked him. But secretly Catrin had to admit that whatever had drawn her to him in the first place was still there, in a lesser degree.

She had recovered from the love affair ten years before by blotting Ashe from her mind. It had been a painful exercise, but eventually it had become second nature never to think of him at all. Yet now, ever since that startling encounter in the hospital, she couldn't help remembering everything that had happened between them. Right up to that last dawn, when he'd kissed her with such ravishing tenderness before he'd left her bed.

Stop it, she thought. None of that. Since Ashe she'd

managed to keep her relationships with men light and undemanding, with no risk to heart or peace of mind. She'd learned her lesson well. Playing with fire was a dangerous pastime, with inevitable, painful consequences. One day she would meet some nice, steady man and settle down to family life. But not yet.

The post came early that Friday. Catrin had opened the door, ready to go to the office, when the postman handed her a bundle of mail. She leafed through them, discarding the usual junk mail, then stared, amused, when she realised the rest were greeting cards. She would have had to be blind not to know it was Valentine's Day, the shops had been full of cards and gifts for weeks, but she hadn't expected to receive any. She opened them in order of size, the first a vast, embarrassing affair with a lace heart and a coy verse. Catrin glowered at it, fairly sure that her married male work colleague was the offender. The second one was humorous, with a short, amusing verse. Julian, she decided, rather touched. When she opened the third her heart missed a beat. It was smaller than the other two, with no verse at all. A miniature watercolour of a single iris was enclosed in a hand-drawn outline of a heart.

Catrin stared at it, standing still in her open doorway.

'My word, who's a popular girl?' said Dinah, coming down the stairs from her flat. 'Three, no less!'

Catrin grinned, and deposited the cards on a table, then locked the door and went down the stairs after her friend. 'Don't tell me Harry didn't send you one this year?'

'I won't. He did.' Dinah smiled smugly. 'In fact my sweet old ex is taking me out to a meal tonight.'

Catrin laughed, shaking her head. 'Some divorce!'

'We're much better friends now we're not married than we were when we were.' Dinah grinned. 'Different arrangements work for different people. Are you going out tonight?'

'Afraid not,' said Catrin cheerfully. 'My admirers just sent cards.'

'Who are they?'

'One of them,' said Catrin, pulling a face, 'should have known better.'

'Ah, the married Lothario.'

'I think so—though I may be doing him an injustice. One of them's from Julian, I think, and the other I'm not sure about.'

Dinah's eyes sparkled. 'I bet you are, really, but you're not telling.'

After an early lunch hour Catrin was hard at work at her desk when the receptionist rang and said there was a man wanting to speak to Miss Hughes.

'Said his name was Ashe—shall I put him through? Catrin—are you there?'

'Yes, right. Sorry, Fiona, I was miles away. Put him on.'

'I've been away,' said Ashe in her ear.

'Really.'

'Yes, really. Medical seminar. How are you, Catrin?'

'Fine.'

'Are you busy?'

'Up to my eyes. How did you know where I worked?'

'Did some sleuthing. I thought I might have more chance of reaching you at work than at home. You're not famous for returning phone calls.'

'Is there something wrong?'

'Not that I know of. I was merely ringing to ask you out over this weekend. You can't keep saying no indefinitely.'

'I'm afraid I can, Ashe,' she said crisply. 'This weekend more than any other. I'm going away.'

'With the man I met last Sunday?'

'No. His job takes him abroad a lot.'

There was silence for a moment, then Ashe said slowly, 'Does that mean you're not involved in a candlelit dinner for two tonight?'

'That's right.' Catrin sighed impatiently. 'Look, Ashe, I've got a lot to get through before I finish tonight—'

'So have I. My first patient's arrived. I'll pick you up at your place at eight.' And without waiting for her reply, Ashe hung up.

Catrin seethed as she tried to concentrate on tax returns. The nerve of the man! Did Ashe really think she was still a pushover, just like the teenager who'd once been so besotted with him? He must learn that he couldn't just snap his fingers and expect her to dance to his tune.

Catrin spent a very irritating evening. Not wishing to eat out on a night when most restaurants were given over to commercial sentimentality, she sent out for a sandwich and ate it at her desk while reading the paperback bestseller she'd bought during her lunch hour. Afterwards she went to a multi-screen cinema and sat through the second half of a screwball comedy, then changed to another section and watched a romantic thriller.

Deciding it was safe to go home at last, Catrin was unsurprised to find no taxis to be had, and trudged home through the rain, feeling murderous towards both Ashe and St Valentine. When she got to Orchard House she was very tired indeed, and in no mood to feel grateful when she found a sheaf of irises lying against her door.

'Where were you?' said the card, which was engraved with the name 'A.S. Hope-Ellison, FRCP'.

Catrin gathered up the flowers and went inside to dump them in the kitchen sink, then looked at the card again. A.S. Hope-Ellison. ASHE. Suddenly she remembered him on the beach, telling her his first name was so gross he never used it. Catrin took off her raincoat and hung it in the bathroom, then went into the kitchen to fill a kettle. Afterwards she switched on the television and sat on the sofa to drink coffee, trying to ignore the winking red light on her telephone. But after a minute or two she gave in, and her mother's voice came into the room, reminding

Catrin that they were expecting her in time for lunch next day. The second message, as she had known it would be, was from Ashe.

'I waited outside in the car for a very long time, Cat. In the end your friend arrived and took charge of the flowers, so I came home. I hope you like them. I had something else for you, too, but I prefer to wait and hand that over in person. Please ring me. I'd like to know you got home safely from wherever you were.'

Suddenly Catrin felt very silly. She'd spent an interminable, boring evening purely to pay Ashe out for his high-handedness. At the time it had seemed important to subject him to a little lesson. Now it just seemed childish.

With a sigh she dialled the number he'd given and heard his recorded voice asking her to leave her name and number. Tit for tat, she thought ruefully, and thanked Ashe politely for the flowers, but made no mention of how she'd spent her evening.

The weekend with Julia and Richard, her stepfather, was a lively occasion, as always when Liam was home, and Catrin enjoyed herself enormously. On the Sunday her grandmother and Hannah and Richard's parents came to lunch, all of them shocked to hear Liam's lurid version of the fire, which was a great deal more bloodthirsty than the toned-down version Catrin had given her mother. On the Sunday evening it was quite a wrench to part from Liam and say goodbye to the others, something Julia was quick to note.

'You need a holiday, darling,' she said, as Richard took Catrin's case to the car.

'I've already had time off to recover from my adventure,' said Catrin with a sigh.

'I mean a holiday, not just time off. You look tired.' Julia smoothed back her daughter's hair to examine the scar under the hall light. 'Hardly noticeable now. Is something wrong?' she added suddenly, fixing her daughter with an X-ray look.

Catrin shook her head. 'No. Nothing. I'm a bit tired, that's all. Anyway, I must be off or I'll miss my train. It's good to see Grandma looking so chirpy. I'll come down again soon. And thanks again for the gorgeous sweater.'

The weekend in the bosom of her family had an unsettling effect on Catrin. For the first half of the week she felt out of sorts and vaguely irritable with life. Then one evening she worked late and emerged from the office into pouring rain and gale-force winds. Gritting her teeth, she turned up the collar of her raincoat, pulled her slouch hat low over her eyes and decided to hotfoot it to the taxi-rank for a ride home. Enough was enough.

Her head was bent so low she didn't see the car cruising along the kerb until it stopped just ahead of her. Ashe jumped out and came round to open the passenger door.

'Hello, Catrin, get in,' he said briskly, and she obeyed, sinking back into the leather seat, too tired to argue.

'Hello, Ashe. Thank you.' She yawned widely. 'I

won't say no on a night like this. I was making for the taxi-rank.'

'Don't you drive?'

'Not worth it in Pennington. I can walk everywhere, and there's a decent train service if I venture farther afield.' Catrin stared through the windscreen at the sluicing rain. 'Why were you in Duke Street?'

'On my way from the hospital I made a detour on the chance of picking up the elusive Miss Hughes. I watched the others leave and thought I'd missed you. You were late.'

She glanced at his profile, surprised. 'You mean you came past on purpose?'

'Yes. Is it so hard to believe?'

'Very. I thought you might have had enough after Friday night.'

'Enough of what?'

'Me, I suppose.'

Ashe slanted her a sideways look, a grim smile at the corners of his mouth. 'Faint heart never won fair maiden.'

Catrin's heart skipped a beat. 'You don't strike me as having a faint heart at any time, Ashe, and I'm certainly no—' She stopped dead.

'Maiden?' he said silkily. 'I know. None better.'

Catrin glared at him, incensed, then her eyes narrowed under the sodden hat-brim. 'You've taken a wrong turning.'

'No. I'm taking you to my home, not yours.'

'But I don't want—'

'Calm down. All I promise is a meal and a talk,

after which I *will* take you home.' Again the sidelong glance. 'You owe me after Friday night.'

True, thought Catrin glumly. Besides, there was nothing to rush home for.

Home to Ashe Hope-Ellison was the entire first floor of one of the spacious old houses typical of Pennington's Regency origins. Catrin liked the deep chairs and the pair of sofas covered in velvet the colour of brandy. That it was a purely masculine home was obvious at first glance, and, after Ashe had taken her wet coat and hat and directed her to a bathroom to tidy up, Catrin examined her pleased reaction to the fact with irritation. It was nothing to her whether Ashe had a woman in his life or not.

With her hair brushed back smoothly into its coil and her face retouched she felt better. Catrin allocated most of her clothes budget to office wear, and she had no qualms about her tailored black suit and cream silk shirt. But her shoes were damp, and Ashe made her sit down and take them off, which rather spoiled the effect.

'I'll stuff them with paper and put them to dry.' He went off with the shoes, looking elegant in a dark suit, his white shirt as pristine as though he'd just put it on, his tie a discreet dark silk. But then, thought Catrin with a pang, Ashe had always looked good whatever he wore. It was the man, not the clothes.

'I like your flat,' she told him when he came back. 'Though I expected you to live in a house.'

'I probably will, one day. When I took the post this was available unfurnished, so I snapped it up.'

'You were lucky,' she said enviously. 'This is a beautiful room. Where do you see your private patients?'

'I share a house nearby with three other consultants.' Ashe looked at her with a wry smile. 'I feel I should open a bottle of champagne to celebrate.'

'Celebrate what?' she asked.

'The fact that I've actually got you here, even if I did have to resort to underhand methods to achieve it.'

Catrin shrugged. 'The weather probably had something to do with it.'

'If it had been a fine night no doubt you'd have walked on by with your nose in the air.'

She looked at him squarely. 'I suppose you think I'm being childish.'

'No.' He held the look. 'I think you can't forgive me.'

'I don't hold a grudge against you.'

'But you don't want to get involved again.'

Only a few days earlier Catrin would have agreed with him. Now she wasn't so sure. 'What I *don't* want is to get hurt again.'

He nodded. 'I can understand that. But now you're actually here, at least let me give you dinner and drive you home.'

She accepted promptly. 'Thank you, I will. I skipped lunch today to avoid working late. There was a flap on, and I promised my boss I'd finish my contribution by tonight.'

'Then have some champagne.' Ashe's smile held a

hint of familiar cajolery, and Catrin found she was no more proof against it now than before.

'One glass,' she said firmly.

Ashe pushed the cork smoothly from the bottle with his thumbs and half filled two flutes. He raised his glass. 'What shall we drink to?'

'A cease-fire?' she suggested dryly.

'By all means—though the only one waging warfare is you, little Cat.'

'Don't call me that,' she said sharply. 'Little Cat grew up, remember. Overnight.'

His face darkened. 'If I could turn back the clock and make things different, I would. I'm trying to make amends—'

'And normally I suppose you don't have to try at all. Where women are concerned, I mean.'

Ashe sat down on one of the sofas, his face set. 'In two particular instances I obviously didn't try hard enough!'

'Let's not talk of personal things,' said Catrin quickly.

Ashe smiled and raised his glass to her. 'Right, then, Catrin. To cessation of hostilities.'

'I'll drink to that,' she agreed, and sipped appreciatively. 'Mmm. Delicious. What are we eating?'

'Does that mean you're hungry?'

'Ravenous.'

'Then follow me.' Ashe led her across the hall into a high-ceilinged kitchen which had very obviously been recently fitted. 'Don't be taken in by the state-of-the-art equipment,' he warned. 'I rarely use any of it, other than the refrigerator and the microwave. Tonight, purely to impress you, I've got something in my spanking new convector oven.'

Catrin sniffed the air appreciatively and chuckled.

'Do that again,' he said softly.

She flushed. 'Do what?'

'Laugh. I was beginning to think you'd forgotten how.'

'I'm normally a very cheerful person,' she retorted. 'But since the fire I've been a bit below par. It's taken time to get back to normal.'

Ashe took silverware and linen napkins from a drawer and handed them to her. 'I sympathise. Though if you hadn't had the accident we might never have met up again. Which would have suited you perfectly, no doubt.'

Catrin made no attempt to deny it as she assembled place-settings beside wood mats on his circular oak table, and added the champagne flutes. Ashe looked at her averted face for a moment, then shrugged and bent to remove a steaming cast-iron pot from the oven. He took off the lid and Catrin sniffed again ecstatically, to lighten the suddenly tense atmosphere.

'It's hot,' he warned, putting it on the table. 'I've got some bread to cut. Do you mind if I take off my jacket?'

Catrin shook her head and removed her own, thinking that Ashe was just as clever as she remembered. Eating together like this in his kitchen was a great deal more intimate than any candlelit dinner for two at an expensive restaurant. Nor had he been tactless enough to have the table ready laid before she came.

He set hot plates at their places, went back for a platter of bread, then sat down and handed her a large ladle. 'Organic lamb, fresh herbs, a hint of garlic, good red wine and various vegetables.'

'I'm impressed!' She helped herself liberally. 'When did you manage to do this?'

He smiled. 'Actually, I didn't. The lady who keeps this place so immaculate put a casserole together for me yesterday. It tastes even better for maturing.'

Catrin ate with relish for a while, then looked at him questioningly. 'This all seems rather premeditated, Ashe. Were you so sure I'd come here tonight?'

'No,' he said shortly. 'Not sure. But I hoped you would. Especially after punishing me by making me wait on Friday.'

'I didn't *make* you wait, Ashe.'

His eyes met hers. 'You knew I would.'

Catrin shrugged. 'I objected to your assumption that I'd be there on command. I'm not a teenager any more, Ashe.'

'I know. You're a very appealing woman, Catrin Hughes.' He topped up their glasses and held up his own in salute.

She coloured slightly, and shook her head when he offered her more bread.

'This man Fellowes,' said Ashe conversationally. 'What is he to you?'

'Just a friend I spend an evening with sometimes.'

'The night, too?'

Catrin glared at him. 'None of your business.'

Ashe took a second helping from the pot. 'If you're in a serious relationship with the man, Catrin, it's very much my business. It's not my habit to trespass on other men's property.'

'I am not Julian's "property", nor anyone else's.'

Ashe nodded in approval. 'Good. I'm happy to hear it.'

'And what about you?' she demanded, pushing her plate away. 'For all I know there could be dozens of women in your life.'

'No damn fear,' he said, laughing. 'Do you think I'm made of money?'

Catrin climbed down from her high horse, smiling reluctantly, then she sobered.

'Now what?' demanded Ashe, eyeing her.

'It occurs to me that I should have said yes.'

'It would certainly be a change from no!'

'I mean I should have said that I *was* in a relationship with Julian.'

His eyes glittered coldly. 'You want me out of your life that much?'

'Not exactly.' She shrugged. 'It's just that I keep suspecting your motives.'

'This is hopeless.' Ashe got up. 'Let's leave all this. Make yourself comfortable in the other room. I'll bring some coffee, then I'll take you home. I apologise for kidnapping you. It was a bad idea.' He held the door for her, his eyes remote, and Catrin went without a word.

Coffee was a long time coming. By the time Ashe

reappeared with a tray Catrin's nerves were on edge. He came in without a word, filled two fragile cups, and handed her one.

'Sugar?' he said politely.

'No, thank you.' Catrin sipped the fiercely strong liquid, glad of the caffeine.

Ashe sat down. 'While I was out there making this,' he began conversationally, 'it occurred to me that perhaps it was time to explain exactly why I've tried so hard to secure a few minutes of your company. It's perfectly simple. Having met up with you again, I want you in my life.'

Catrin stared at him, the cup halfway to her lips. 'I don't understand.'

He gave her a derisive smile. 'Oh, come on, Catrin. You're not a teenager any more. You know exactly what I mean.'

She drank the rest of her coffee, set the cup down with delicate precision. 'You mean all this—the flowers, the card, the phone calls—is just a means of getting me to bed?'

'Of course not. I won't lie and say bed isn't part of what I want, but not all of it.' He shrugged. 'I intended to wait longer, made the approach slower and more subtle, but seeing you across the dinner table, sharing a meal with you, I realise that the attraction you had for me before is still there, more mature, and even more compelling for that. I don't know why. I've known a lot of women in the past ten years, Catrin—'

'Then I suggest you revert to one of them,' she

snapped and jumped to her feet. 'May I use your phone, please?'

'No. I said I'll drive you home and I will.' He rose to bar her way. 'But before I do there's something I need to know.'

Catrin stood very still, wishing she had her shoes on. 'What is it?' she said suspiciously.

'This.' Ashe pulled her up on tiptoe, and kissed her.

Catrin tried to control her response, to remain rigid as he smoothed a hand down her spine, but it was useless. Ten years vanished in the blink of an eye, and she was eighteen and a clamouring mass of responses to the man whose kiss was so overwhelmingly different from any other man's. One touch of his lips, his hands, and she felt desire wrench at her, beset by feelings no other man had ever come near to arousing. Shocked by her own response, she pulled away, and Ashe set her back on her feet, grasping her by the elbows to keep her steady as she blinked up owlishly into his intent face.

'So it's still there,' he said, his eyes glittering.

Catrin nodded, knowing it was useless to deny it.

'What shall we do about it?'

'Do?'

'I told you I wanted you, Catrin. I wanted you the minute I set eyes on you all those years ago on the beach. You were all eyes and mouth and long dark hair. And trying so hard not to be shy. It took every shred of control I possessed to go slow with you.' His voice was harsh with suppressed emotion.

What was it? thought Catrin. Regret? Lust? 'I

wasn't so shy in the end. I was the one who asked you to kiss me, even suggested we went to bed.' She shook her head impatiently. 'Why are we resurrecting all this? We can't go back—'

'But we could go forward, Catrin.' Ashe came behind her and slid his arms round her waist. 'We're adults now. There's no impediment to this.' Slowly he slid his fingers upwards over the silk, and she tensed as his cupping hands drew her closer. His fingertips sent fire streaking from his touch to every part of her body, and she felt him harden against her, his lips hot on the nape of her neck. Then he plucked the pins from her coiled hair and ran his fingers through it before turning her in his arms. Her face flamed as his eyes dropped to the twin evidence of her arousal, clearly visible against the silk of her shirt, and she hugged her arms around her chest, shaking her head emphatically.

'No, Ashe.'

His jaw clenched. 'Why not? The chemistry's still there.'

'I know. But I'm not eighteen any more. Neither,' she added bluntly, 'do I do anything about contraception these days.'

Ashe regarded her in silence for a moment, visibly controlling the passion which had almost mastered him a few moments before. 'I'm prepared for that, Catrin.'

'Are you, indeed?' She pushed her hair away from her face. 'I may have been a pushover ten years ago, Ashe, but I've grown up a bit since then. It takes more than a glass of champagne and a pleasant dinner these days.'

'Then what does it take?' he asked cuttingly.

Catrin shrugged. 'I'm old-fashioned. Men don't need to wrap up their requirements in sentiment, I know, but for me it's different. I made love with you all those years ago solely because I was so madly *in* love with you.'

'Are you saying you feel nothing at all for me now?' he demanded.

'No.' She sighed. 'You know how to press the right buttons. For a moment there I was almost ready to give in. But where you're concerned my main feeling is wariness, Ashe. I knew I was playing with fire last time. No way am I getting burnt again.'

CHAPTER EIGHT

ASHE looked at her in silence for so long Catrin had to force herself not to fidget.

'I was a fool,' he said bitterly, at last. 'I rushed things.'

She shrugged. 'On the contrary, you've been very patient up to now, sending me flowers and so on.'

'I told you. I want us to be friends. But I also intend to be your lover again.' He smiled suddenly, the gleam in his eyes very familiar.

'You seem very confident!' she said tartly.

He shook his head. 'It's a simple matter of kismet, Catrin. Why waste the second chance fate has thrown our way? I would have expected you to be married by now. As you are not, and neither am I now—'

'How long since your divorce?' she interrupted.

'Ten years.' His mouth twisted. 'The marriage was over before I met you, Catrin. It was so brief, sometimes I forget I ever had a wife—but you don't want to hear about that.'

'Actually, I do,' said Catrin firmly. 'If you meant what you said about being friends.'

'More than just friends,' he warned.

'Don't rush me!' She looked at him in appeal. 'What I'm trying to say is that I need to know what happened back then. With your wife. Why you didn't tell me you were married.'

Ashe took her by the hand and led her to a sofa. 'Let's sit down. But remember it's a long time ago. I haven't thought about Monica in years.'

Catrin settled herself beside him, leaving her hand in his. 'Did she remarry?'

'As soon as the divorce came through, much to my relief.' Ashe's grasp tightened. 'We met when she joined the hospital administration staff. She was sexy, good-looking, older—and cunning. When she told me she was pregnant I felt obliged to do the decent thing and married her. Shortly afterwards I found she'd lied. Doctor or not, I'd fallen for the oldest scam in the book.'

'So what did you do?'

'Tried to make a go of it. But it was impossible. I worked punishingly long hours and I was also study-ing for exams. But it turned out that Monica had mar-ried me in the mistaken idea that my family was loaded. When she discovered I had only my salary to live on she was off like a shot to pastures new.'

'What did you do?'

Ashe shrugged. 'I threw myself into work, passed the exams which officially made me a member of the Royal College of Physicians, and eventually went down to Pembrokeshire alone on the holiday I'd booked for a delayed honeymoon.'

Catrin was silent for a moment. 'So that's why you looked so haggard. I thought you were recovering from some illness or other.'

'I was, in a way. And for a short, blissful interlude you provided the cure.' Ashe smiled fleetingly. 'For the wounds Monica inflicted, at least. I've never recovered from the blow of losing *you*.'

Catrin wanted passionately to believe him. 'Were you going to tell me about that over the dinner we never had back then?' she asked, her eyes on their clasped hands.

'Yes,' he said, and looked down at her. 'I was going to ask you to wait for me until my divorce was through. Until you had your degree, if you wanted. But make no mistake, Catrin, if *you'd* told me you were pregnant I'd have married you the minute I was free.'

'I couldn't have told you,' she pointed out. 'I had no idea where you'd gone.'

'Then you *were* pregnant,' he pounced.

'I was not!' She pulled her hand from his grasp. 'Don't you ever give up, Ashe? Liam is not your son.'

'Then why in hell does he look so much like me?' Ashe demanded.

'He doesn't. He looks like his father. The man my mother's married to,' said Catrin in desperation. 'We just happen to have a similar taste in men—' She stopped, flushing at the sudden gleam in his eyes.

'Then you don't deny I'm to your taste, Catrin!'

'No, I suppose not.' She stared at him defiantly. 'But that doesn't mean I'm ready to risk a love affair with you, Ashe.'

'Why should it be a risk?' he demanded.

'I haven't forgotten what happened last time,' she

retorted, then gave a sudden, involuntary yawn. 'Sorry. I'm tired. Don't bother to drive me home. Just call a cab.'

'Certainly not.'

Catrin gave a tired little shrug of agreement. 'Whatever you say. But I really am tired, Ashe. I want to go home.'

'In a minute,' he promised. 'I have something for you. I mentioned it during one of the phone messages I'm always leaving for you.'

Ashe went out of the room, and came back with a large envelope. He held it out to her. 'These are copies. I thought you might like them as a keepsake.'

Catrin took a bundle of snapshots from the envelope, her heart missing a beat as she realised they were mostly shots of herself. Only a few of them were of Ashe, taken on the rare occasions when she'd captured his camera from him that long-ago summer. The sight of their tanned, laughing faces brought back their passionate encounter so vividly that she was unable to speak for a moment.

'I'd forgotten about your camera,' she said huskily at last. 'How young we look.'

'When I left I was in such a state I threw the camera in the glove compartment of the car and forgot about it. Even when I sold the car. Eventually, when the new owner found the camera and posted it back to me, I had the film developed.' Ashe sat down beside her, looking over her shoulder at the prints. 'One look at that shy smile was enough to start me searching for you, desperate to see you again at all costs.'

'And now you have,' said Catrin soberly. 'But we're different people from these two, Ashe.'

'The only difference is age. The pull between us is just the same.' Ashe turned her face towards him. 'Given the chance it could be even stronger, now we've matured a little along the way.' He kissed her very lightly, then got up. 'Right, Catrin. Time you were in bed. Yours, alas, not mine. I'll drive you home.'

'I'll take you out for a meal tomorrow night,' he said, when they arrived at Orchard House. 'And this time I expect you to be ready and waiting when I come.'

That night, Catrin would realise later, was a turning point in her life.

Dinah was impressed. 'Are things hotting up between you two?' she asked during the weekend.

'Not exactly. We're just spending a bit more time together. No big deal,' said Catrin casually.

'How about Julian?'

'I'll have to put him on hold for a while.'

Dinah laughed. 'And how will he take that?'

Catrin grinned. 'I don't know. Watch this space.'

'Does he know about Ashe?'

'He's met him.'

'And?'

'They didn't exactly hit it off.'

Dinah gurgled. 'How wonderful! It's a long time since I had a couple of blokes scrapping over me.'

'I wouldn't put it quite like that,' laughed Catrin,

though secretly she decided it was only human to feel the tiniest bit gratified.

Wary at first, after a while Catrin relaxed enough to enjoy the time spent with Ashe: walks in the country, trips to the theatre, dining out in restaurants—though there were no more meals at his flat, nor did she invite him to supper at hers.

'Why?' he demanded one night, when he drove her home.

'Because it's best, for the time being anyway, that we keep to neutral ground. If we get too—too involved, it will be harder to get back to normal when this is over.'

Ashe killed the engine and turned to her urgently. 'It doesn't have to be over. Can't you get it through your head, Cat? I want you on a permanent basis. I'll buy a house if you'll move in with me.'

'No. Please. I'm not ready for that.' She looked down at her clasped hands. 'But I appreciate your patience, Ashe, about rushing—or not rushing—me to bed.'

'I'm glad my noble restraint hasn't gone unnoticed,' he said dryly.

'How long will it last?'

'As long as it takes.' He leaned over and kissed her mouth. 'But don't make me wait too long, Catrin. We've wasted enough time already.'

'You can't look on it as wasted.' She smiled up into his eyes. 'You've been busy climbing the medical ladder and I've been slogging away at becoming a chartered accountant.'

'Since we could have been together and still achieved all that it still seems like time wasted to me!'

Catrin made no mention of Ashe to her mother during her next visit to Stratford. Ashe was someone she needed to keep to herself now as much as she had ten years before. No matter how much he declared he wanted a permanent relationship, Catrin couldn't help holding back. She was in love with him again, she admitted to herself. Or perhaps she was *still* in love with him and had never stopped. And this, really, was the stumbling block. If she gave in to Ashe and moved in with him, as he wanted her to, it would make things so impossibly difficult when they broke up.

When, she thought, not if. Which was odd. Why was she so sure that sharing her life with Ashe was fraught with danger?

Eventually, as Catrin had fully expected, Ashe grew impatient with the confines she was placing on their relationship. They had made the most of early March sunshine one Sunday, driving into the Cotswolds for a pub lunch and going for a walk afterwards before heading back for home.

They were on top of a hill, looking down on Broadway, when Ashe turned to her suddenly. 'This is driving me mad, Catrin. We're two adults in an exclusive relationship, but you won't commit yourself to me.'

'You mean I won't go to bed with you!'

'That too.' Ashe turned away, hands in the pockets of his suede jacket. He stared down unseeingly at the view below. 'I won't pretend I don't want that—sometimes so much it's all I can do not to act the caveman and force you into bed. Which, of course, is why you veto any time spent at my place. Or yours.'

'Yes,' admitted Catrin honestly. 'It is. I wanted to be sure before—'

'Sure of what, for heaven's sake!' He turned on her, his eyes glittering in a way which made her back a little. 'You might well retreat,' he said through his teeth. 'Only the fact that we're visible for miles, and a fair amount of other people are in the vicinity, is preserving your safety, Catrin Hughes.'

'Then it's time we went,' she snapped, and started down the way they'd just climbed.

Ashe followed her swiftly, and in simmering silence they completed the descent and returned to his car.

Once inside, Catrin turned to him. 'It isn't working, is it?' she demanded.

'No.' Ashe made no pretence of misunderstanding. 'I thought I could be patient, but, dammit, Cat, I'm not a randy schoolboy, dangling after you for a spot of fun and games. I'm an adult and I want an adult relationship where we live together and, yes, sleep together, too. When a man loves a woman it's a fairly normal thing for him to want.'

Catrin looked at him, startled.

'Now what?' he demanded impatiently.

'You've made no mention of actual feelings up to now,' she said quietly.

Ashe relaxed a little, looking thoughtful. 'No,' he said, at last, as though he'd been looking back at the times they'd spent together. 'I suppose I haven't. I thought it was obvious. Of course I love you, Cat. I did all those years ago, too. That's why it was such a hell of a blow when—'

'When you *thought* you saw me in a car with someone else.' She slanted a look at him. 'You subjected me to a lot of grief. *You* made the mistake. But I paid for it.'

'What do you mean?' He swivelled in his seat to look at her.

'I mean you caused me a lot of secret tears, that's all. Nothing more sinister.' She smiled a little. 'I've been wary ever since of getting too close to any man. Not,' she added with candour, 'that I've been tempted too much until—'

'Until?' he prompted.

'Until I met you again.'

Ashe gazed at her in triumph. 'So why the hell are you keeping me waiting, Catrin? Punishment?'

'No.' She frowned. 'I suppose I was waiting until the time was right.'

'And when will that be? This year, next year?'

Catrin made no reply, and with jaw clenched Ashe drove off in silence. He maintained it all the way back to Pennington, and she made no move to break it, because the one thing Ashe wanted her to say wasn't possible. She just wasn't ready to give in to him yet, despite his casual declaration of love. Suspicious she might be, but she had a feeling the words of love had not been casual at all, but spoken specifically to get his own way.

When they arrived at her flat Catrin thanked him politely for a pleasant day. Ashe looked at her morosely, said goodbye, then drove off before she'd even put her key in the outer door. Which was a surprise. Somehow she'd expected him to ask to come in and continue with the earlier conversation. Which, she thought, more than once during the ensuing evening, served her right for taking Ashe for granted.

Catrin wouldn't have admitted it to a soul, but as the week wore on with no word from Ashe she became worried. Every night when she left the office she looked for his car in vain. And when she got home, if there was a red light on her answering machine, the message was never from Ashe. She was on the point of ringing his flat several times, but at the last minute drew back. If she made contact he would naturally assume she was ready and willing to do what he asked. But by the time Friday arrived, and still no word from Ashe, Catrin *was* ready and willing to say yes to anything he wanted. The feeling lasted for a whole evening, then finally anger took over. If this was the way he wanted it, fine. Two could play at that game. She rang her mother and asked if she could come down for the weekend, and received the usual, delighted response.

Catrin caught an early train next day, and began to relax, looking forward to two whole days of neither seeing Ashe, nor expecting to hear from him. As always, the time passed swiftly with Julia and Richard. They had friends round for dinner on the Saturday night, and Catrin helped her mother prepare and serve the meal, and enjoyed the relaxed, undemanding evening. Next day there was a walk, followed by a drink at the local before lunch, then a long, lazy afternoon in front of the fire before Catrin reluctantly packed her belongings in time to catch the train.

Just as they were ready to leave a phone call delayed Richard for a few minutes, then on the way into Stratford they encountered a road accident, with police directing traffic. Richard drove into the station at last just in time to see the Pennington train pulling out.

'Never mind, love, I'll drive you home,' he said cheerfully. 'It's not far.' He took out his cellphone to ring Julia, explained briefly, and they were on their way.

It took less than an hour to reach Pennington, but Richard refused to come in for coffee before getting back to Julia. He gave Catrin his usual bear hug, kissed her soundly, then ran back to the car. Catrin waved him off, picked up her case and went up the smooth stone stairs, scowling at the pineapple as she went. She was barely through the door when her intercom buzzed, and she picked up the receiver, thinking Richard must have forgotten something.

Her heart gave a thump when she found it was Ashe, his voice harsh as he demanded to see her.

Catrin deliberately let him wait a moment or two.

'All right. Come up.' She pressed the button to release the outer door, took off her raincoat, then opened the door to Ashe's peremptory knock.

'Who is he?' he demanded, coming into the room like a whirlwind.

'Who do you mean?' she said, backing away involuntarily, but he seized her by the shoulders, staring down into her face.

'How many men kiss you goodbye on your doorstep? I *mean* the man I just saw you with.'

Catrin tried to push him away, but Ashe's fingers bit deeper. She glared at him, incensed. 'Not that it's any business of yours, but it was Richard—'

'Who the hell's Richard?'

'My stepfather—'

'Your *stepfather*?' Ashe stared at her in disbelief, then pulled her into his arms and began to kiss her: hard, bruising kisses, nothing to do with love.

Catrin struggled, pushing at him, but Ashe had been drinking, she realised in sudden alarm. He wasn't drunk, but he wasn't completely sober, either. Normally he rarely drank more than a glass or two of wine, and suddenly she felt afraid.

'Yes,' he said, against her mouth. 'I've been drinking. I went to lunch at the house of one of my colleagues. Very nice. Sunday lunch with the family. A roast and good red wine and a brandy afterwards. I walked home, then decided to have another brandy, because the comfortable, untidy domesticity I'd just experienced, complete with squabbling children and a pair of muddy dogs, made me miss you so much it hurt.'

He thrust her away so abruptly Catrin rocked on her heels. 'So I had a third brandy, and in the end, like a lovesick fool, I took a taxi here, determined to see you, tired of my waiting game. I'd forced myself to stay away from you all week, but suddenly I couldn't wait another minute to see you. So I came and rang your doorbell. But no Catrin. After a while I gave up and decided to walk home for the second time in one day. I was halfway along the street when I turned back to see a car drawing up.' He stared down at her. 'Was that really your stepfather?'

'Yes.'

'He's younger than I expected. And from where I was standing a damn sight too fond of his stepdaughter.'

'Don't be disgusting,' she snapped with distaste.

Ashe moved swiftly and pulled her into his arms again. 'I was jealous. Why the hell do I want you so much?'

'Why ask me?' she retorted, trying to stay unmoved. 'Because I won't say yes, perhaps?'

'You think you've got me on a piece of string,' he said softly, eyes narrowed. 'All this is great fun for you, Cat, isn't it?'

'All what?'

'Keeping me at arm's length. Punishing me for past sins.'

'It isn't *fun*,' she said angrily. 'It's a safety measure. If you don't like it, you know what to do.'

'Yes, I do,' he agreed bitterly, and to her dismay turned on his heel and went through the door, closing it behind him so quietly it shocked her more than if he'd slammed it shut with all his might.

For a moment she stood still, rooted to the floor, then she ran for the door and went careering down the stairs after him, skidding on the last three, and he spun round to catch her.

'Don't go,' she said hoarsely, her heart banging against her ribs, fear of losing him again far greater than her fear of falling.

Ashe set her safe on the second step, so that her eyes were on a level with his. 'Why do you want me to stay?' he demanded, releasing her.

'Because I've missed you,' she said flatly. 'Have you been staying away to punish *me*?'

'Yes. Did I succeed?'

She nodded. 'I almost rang you several times, but I was too—'

'Obstinate to give in?'

'No. I was afraid you might tell me to go away. That you'd had enough of my delaying tactics.'

'I had,' he said, taking her breath away.

'So why did you come here tonight?' she said, stung.

'Because, like any mature adult male in full control of his life, I couldn't damn well keep away.' He shrugged. 'Laugh, if you want to.'

She shook her head. 'I'm not laughing. Come back upstairs with me. Please?'

Ashe regarded her in silence, and moved a fraction

closer. Her disobedient pulse quickened in instant response to the male scent of him, the soap he used, the heathery smell of his light tweed jacket mingled with the tang of the brandy he'd drunk, even the dark shadow along his jaw, where he needed his second shave of the day.

'I thought your flat was off-limits,' he said without expression.

Catrin gave up. No way was she going to plead with him. With a shrug she turned away, but Ashe caught her by the shoulders and turned her back to him.

'I would like very much to come up,' he said very deliberately. 'It would be very pleasant just to sit and talk, drink coffee, even watch television together. The kind of things you've ruled out over the past weeks because you don't trust me to be in the same room without leaping on you and demanding your body.'

'Those weren't my reasons!' she said, aghast. 'I didn't want you in my place because—'

'Because you thought I'd be bound to want to take you to bed.'

'No, Ashe.' She gave him a wry little smile. 'It's very simple. I had quite a fight to recover when you vanished ten years ago. So I've been keeping my flat off-limits because I like living here. I don't want to move to make it easier to get over you again. Afterwards.'

'I think I had better come up,' he said, and walked up the stairs beside her. 'We have things to discuss I'd rather not go into in your hallway.'

Catrin ushered him into the flat and waved him to her sofa. 'Would you like some coffee?'

'Not just this minute. I'd rather continue with the conversation we were having downstairs.' He patted the cushions beside him. 'Come and sit here. And tell me why in hell you're so certain any relationship of ours is bound to come to an end. Admittedly I was an idiot first time round, but this time, Cat, it will be different, I promise you. I've given up jumping to the wrong conclusions.'

'You did with Richard tonight,' she reminded him.

Ashe gave her a crooked smile. 'I'm human enough to object if I find you in another man's arms, Catrin.'

'So what do we do now?' she asked after a moment.

'Drink this coffee you promised me. It might dispel the last lingering effects of my unaccustomed brandy binge.' He grinned at her and Catrin relaxed, light-headed with relief.

She reached up and kissed him lightly on the mouth. 'Right. But no food, I'm afraid; I need to go shopping—what's the matter?'

'Nothing. I'm just recovering from the shock of the first voluntary kiss you've ever given me.' He reached for her and pulled her onto his lap. 'Do it again.'

Catrin smiled and obliged with an ardour that Ashe reacted to predictably, his arms tightening as he returned the kiss with interest. He rubbed his cheek against her hair, then began loosening it, dismantling the neat coil until the glossy strands fell to her shoulders. He ran his fingers through it, then cupped her face in his hands.

'Let's forget the coffee,' he said huskily. 'If you go off to make it, how can I be sure you'll be in the same frame of mind when you come back?'

'I don't want any coffee either,' she muttered against his throat, and Ashe brought her face round to his, looking deep into her eyes.

'Does this mean you've had a change of heart, Catrin?' he asked very gravely.

'No. I've wanted this all along. Just now, when you walked out, I realised how I'd feel if you never came back.'

'And how would you feel?' he asked, breathing faster.

Catrin's eyes glittered suddenly with unshed tears. 'Like I felt the last time. As though the world had ended.'

CHAPTER NINE

ASHE drew her close, burying his face in her hair, for once so obviously at a loss for words that any last defences Catrin possessed melted away. She burrowed against him, still shaky from the shock of having him walk out, and he turned her face up to his, kissing away the tears, then kissing her mouth with a tenderness which brought everything into sudden perspective for Catrin. She slid from his lap, her eyes luminous with invitation as she held out her hand to him. Ashe was right. Fate had brought them together for a purpose. They had been meant to meet again. And to love again.

She told him so as they sank down on her bed together, and Ashe shook his head, smoothing a long finger down her cheek.

'Not *again* exactly, sweetheart. For years I'd persuaded myself I'd forgotten you, but one look at the Catrin I recognised behind the dressing and the bruises, and I knew I'd never stopped loving you, let alone forgotten you.' He smiled crookedly. 'Which would have been rather inconvenient if a large, possessive husband had turned up at visiting time.'

Catrin giggled. 'Julian came, with orchids.'

Ashe growled something very uncomplimentary about Julian and kissed her fiercely, demanding a response she gave so unstintingly they were soon undressing each other feverishly, their caressing hands urgent with the intensity of feeling that swamped them both. They came together in a fury of longing which swept the years away and transported them back in time to experience the same amazing, blazing rapture that neither of them had ever hoped to find again.

'I thought I'd imagined it,' he said hoarsely at last, and raised his head to look at her. 'I told myself I was looking back at the past through rose-coloured glasses, that it couldn't possibly have been the way I remembered it. But it was. It still is.'

'Only with you, though,' said Catrin, and his eyes darkened.

'Does that mean you tried to find it with someone else?'

She nodded.

'I don't want to know,' he said gruffly.

'Don't you?'

'Yes, dammit, I do,' he groaned.

'In college I had loads of male friends, but no boyfriend. Which was a challenge to some men, it's true, but I was never even tempted. Then I went skiing to Zermatt one year with friends. I met a young English ski-guide, blond, tanned, ex-Oxford, about to be something in the City. He was very good-looking, fun to be with, and he pursued me relentlessly. So, out of sheer curiosity, I let him catch me one night.'

Ashe slid his hands into her hair, staring down into her eyes. 'And?'

'It was not a success.'

'In what way?'

Her eyes glittered gold in the lamplight. 'When it came to the push I just couldn't do it—still hung up on you.' She smiled ruefully. 'He was a very good sport about it, too.'

'And since?' he demanded harshly.

'Are you going to confess every last one of your encounters since we last met?' she demanded.

'No,' he said shortly. 'You're right. Let's forget the years between and just remember how lucky we are to find each other again.'

'Amen to that.' She looked up at him drowsily. 'It's getting late.'

'Do you want me to go?'

'No.' She stretched against him and his eyes dilated. 'You could get a taxi first thing in the morning, I suppose. Shall we postpone the coffee I mentioned until breakfast?'

Ashe didn't even bother to reply, her final words smothered with kisses which swiftly brought about the same, overwhelming conclusion, both of them fired with a mutual need to make up for the years spent apart.

He left her in a cold, wet dawn, and Catrin watched him go downstairs, waiting until he turned at the first landing to wave before she retreated and closed the door. This was the first day of the rest of her life, she thought happily, as she went to run a bath. And life was wonderful. Ashe had told her he loved her so often during the night that she had no more qualms about the future. Nor the past.

The one snag to the new way of things was Ashe's demand that she give up her flat and move in with him.

'I'd like to stay as we are for a while,' she said, a few evenings later in his flat.

'Afraid to burn your boats in case I disappear again?' he demanded.

'No. Not that. But this is all so new. I want time to savour it before we make any changes.' She reached up to kiss him. 'Don't be angry with me.'

He smiled at her crookedly. 'When you look at me like that it's very difficult to be angry with you, as you know very well.'

'I just want to get used to us as—'

'Lovers?'

'All right, lovers. I like having you ring me, and call for me, and all those things that don't happen once people live together.'

Ashe's smile was openly indulgent. 'I forget, sometimes, that you're younger. Of course I'll wait. But not too long, Cat, please. In fact,' he added, 'shouldn't you be taking me to visit your family some time, in the usual way? My parents are no longer with us, unfortunately, or I'd be only too glad to show you off to them. They would have loved you.'

She rubbed her cheek against his. 'I expect Mother will take to you, too, Ashe.'

'How about Richard?' he asked dryly.

Catrin sat up. 'Why shouldn't Richard like you?

Don't tell me you're still harbouring dark thoughts about him just because you saw him hugging me the other night?'

'No! It's just this damnable jealousy thing where you're concerned. You're the only woman I've ever met who brings it out in me.' Ashe pulled her onto his lap. 'Are you going to tell your mother we've met before?'

'I'll have to. I mentioned your name quite a lot back then. She's bound to remember it.' Catrin leaned nearer to kiss him and Ashe held her close, elated, as always, by any unsolicited caress from her. Eventually she drew away, smiling up at him mischievously. 'You've never told me what your name actually is, by the way. Perhaps I should have waited to find out before committing myself.'

He sighed heavily. 'Are you sure you want to know? I've been Ashe ever since my first day in school, from my initials. I fought like a maniac if anyone used my first name.'

'What is it, for heaven's sake?'

'My parents saw fit to christen me Aubrey St John Hope-Ellison. You have my full permission to laugh,' he added.

Catrin bit back a giggle. 'I prefer Ashe,' she admitted. 'Is it a family name?'

'St John was my mother's maiden name, and Aubrey was by way of great expectations, after a rich uncle,' he said gloomily. 'The old devil left me a couple of bad oil paintings and a fob watch when he died, but the rest of his money went to charity.'

'Oh, bad luck,' she sympathised, trying to keep her voice steady.

'Are you laughing at me?'

'What'll happen if I do?'

'Try it and find out!'

Catrin's punishment was so much to her liking that it was a long time before Ashe returned to the subject of her family.

'Why not ring them now, and ask if we can visit them this weekend?'

She looked at him, frowning. 'Why the rush?'

Ashe pushed her hair back from her face, his eyes holding hers. 'I have this feeling that if we don't make things official in some way as soon as possible all this will vanish in a puff of smoke.'

She smiled, touched. 'All right. Hand me the phone.'

Julia, as was obvious from the first word she uttered, was in no condition to receive visitors that weekend. 'I've got a filthy cold, darling,' she said regretfully. 'And I've passed it on to Richard. And this weekend would have been out anyway, because we were due to take Liam out on Sunday. It's one of his days off, but we've had to cancel. Come next week instead.'

Catrin promised, ordered her parent to take all possible remedies, sent her love to her sneezing stepfather, then rang off to explain to Ashe.

'I'm sorry your mother's ill.' He looked at her enquiringly. 'What was that about Liam?'

'It's his Sunday off. Richard was driving Mother over to take him out for lunch.'

'We could take him instead,' he said casually.

Catrin eyed him with suspicion. 'Why would you want to do that?'

'Because Liam will be done out of his treat otherwise.' His eyes challenged her. 'Are you afraid to let me near him?'

'Of course not.' She looked at him in silence for a moment, then shrugged. 'All right. I'll ring Mother again and tell her to arrange it.'

The mention of Liam had brought a faint constraint into the atmosphere, and when Catrin said she wanted to go home a few minutes later Ashe did nothing to detain her. He stopped the car outside her flat, and turned to her.

'Look, Catrin, if you'd prefer we didn't take Liam out on Sunday, just say the word.'

'I've arranged it with Mother now,' she pointed out. 'Besides, it might be a good thing if you did experience a few hours of keeping Liam amused. Be warned—he can be exhausting. And he eats like a horse.'

'So you don't mind?'

'Why should I mind?' she said carelessly. 'You'll earn Brownie points with Mother, so that's all to the good for future harmony.'

'Nevertheless, I sense a chill.'

'If you do, you know why,' she said impatiently. 'Hanker after Liam as much as you like; he's not your son, Ashe.'

'I should know that by now. You've told me often enough,' Ashe retorted.

'Ah, but do you really believe me?'

'Yes,' he said shortly.

'I wish I could believe *you*. Don't get out,' she added quickly.

'But I'm not going to see you until Saturday,' he objected.

'You enjoy your medical dinner tomorrow night, and I'll enjoy my cinema outing with the girls on Friday,' she said firmly. 'It's good to keep other interests.'

'Am I allowed a goodnight kiss?' he said sardonically.

Catrin smiled at him, and held up her face. 'As many as you like.'

'Then let me come up with you—'

'No chance. I really must have an early night, and my powers of resistance tend to be nil when you kiss me, Ashe, as you know very well.'

'Remind me of that next time we're in private!' He reached for her and kissed her at length, tipping her head back so he could move his lips down her throat, and she shivered and somewhere found the will to push him away.

'You see what I mean!' she said breathlessly. 'Goodnight, Ashe.'

'I'll call you,' he promised as she slid from the car.

Ashe was as good as his word. He spoke to her at length when she was in bed each night, some of his conversation doing little to aid sleep. Catrin, well aware that Ashe knew exactly what he was doing, nevertheless grew more and more of a mind to move in with him. She was reluctant to leave the flat she'd taken over from her aunt, nor did she much care for the idea of moving into Ashe's place. Somewhere new was the obvious solution, and she told Ashe so when he arrived on the Saturday evening.

'Let's not go out tonight,' she said as she took his coat. 'I've cooked a meal.'

'That's music to my ears,' he sighed, sinking down on the sofa. 'I've had a hectic couple of days. One of my private patients got the time wrong and didn't turn up until seven last night. By the time I'd given him a going over and told him he was in need of an endoscopy I was a bit weary. My Outpatients clinic at the hospital was a bit protracted today, too. Sorry,' he added, and held out his hand. 'Come and sit down and tell me how much you've missed me.'

'I have,' she assured him. 'Why didn't you tell me about the endoscopy last night—whatever it is?'

He grinned. 'I was trying to woo you, sweetheart. Talk of a patient swallowing a camera on a tube wouldn't have furthered my cause much!'

Catrin shuddered. 'You're right!' She looked at him in silence for a moment. He wore a cashmere sweater the exact colour of his eyes, and suddenly she wanted him to kiss her so badly he knew it, and pulled her into his arms.

'It won't always be like this,' he said unevenly after a while. 'In a few years' time we'll be squabbling and taking each other for granted.'

'I can't imagine that,' she whispered.

'Neither can I!' Ashe pushed her away gently. 'We'd better eat this dinner, before I get completely out of hand.'

Catrin kissed him swiftly on the cheek, then went to fetch a corkscrew. 'You open the wine you brought last time, and I'll bring the supper in.'

Catrin's kitchen was too small for two to eat in it, and apart from her bedroom the only other room in the flat was her large living room. While Ashe poured the wine she made up two plates with asparagus tips, buttered potatoes and chicken breasts baked with leeks, bacon and mushrooms in filo pastry.

'Wonderful,' said Ashe, after the first mouthful.

'Mother gave me the recipe. She's a fan of TV cooking programmes.' Catrin smiled at him. 'But it would be better at a table. Which brings me to the subject I want to discuss tonight.'

Ashe looked at her questioningly. 'Are you feeding me so exquisitely just to soften a blow of some kind?'

She shook her head. 'I thought I might bring up the subject of living together.'

He swallowed suddenly, and coughed, then took a mouthful of wine, looking at her in astonishment. 'I'm the one who harps on that particular subject, not you, sweetheart. Have you changed your mind? Are you actually going to move into the flat with me?'

'No—'

'You want me to come here?' he said, surprised.

'No to that, too. I thought we might look at something new to both of us. A house, maybe. If you're still of the same mind,' she added hastily.

Ashe drank down the rest of his wine, his eyes glittering. 'Oh, yes, Catrin. I'm still of the same mind. We'll start looking next week, before you change yours.'

'Good.' She smiled demurely. 'There's an estate agent next to my office. I had a peep in there yesterday.'

Ashe shook his head. 'Can this be the lady who wouldn't even have dinner with me not so long ago? Why the U-turn?'

'Simple. You told me you love me. Before that I thought you just wanted to bed me. Love, Ashe, was the element missing with the other men I've known—'

'How many?' he demanded, suddenly pale.

'Not many at all. And I didn't mean ''known'' in the biblical sense, Ashe. In all these years I've only tried to make love with the ski-instructor I told you about. And a very nice male colleague in the firm I used to work for. He wanted to marry me, but when it came to the bed part it was a disaster. It was impossible to go on working together afterwards so I applied for other jobs. And here I am.' Catrin got up and collected his plate. 'I'm not even going to ask about *your* experiences over the years. What's the point?'

Ashe got up and followed her into the kitchen. He waited until she put the plates in the sink, then drew her into his arms. 'There haven't been that many, Catrin. And believe me, darling, I never misled any lady about my intentions. I learned my lesson with Monica. By the time I met you again I'd resigned myself to a bachelor existence. But now...' He kissed her before going on. 'Now, Catrin Hughes, I can't imagine life without you.'

Ashe called for her early next morning and Catrin was ready and waiting, attired in her favourite chocolate wool office suit, with her hair tied back with a brown ribbon instead of the usual neat coil she wore to work.

'You look very elegant,' he said, kissing her. 'Am I smart enough?'

Catrin surveyed his suede jacket and roll-neck sweater with approval. 'Absolutely. Not too formal. I'm sure Liam will approve.'

'I used to hate it if my parents looked the slightest bit out of the ordinary when they came to see me.' He grinned. 'How about you?'

'I went to a day school, Ashe,' she said matter-of-factly. 'Days out weren't part of my life. Anyway, it doesn't really matter what *we* wear—we're not parents.'

There was an odd little silence.

'No,' said Ashe slowly. 'We're not. Could we be, perhaps?'

Her eyes flashed angrily. 'If you're going to keep harping—'

'I *meant*,' he said swiftly, 'would you want children one day? Our children.'

'Oh.' Catrin simmered down. 'Well, yes, I suppose so.'

'You don't sound too enthusiastic!'

She flushed a little. 'Only because I hadn't thought of it before.'

'You might give it some consideration,' he said dryly. 'Time's ticking by, Catrin. And we've wasted a damn sight too much of it already.'

The day was fine, with spring in the air, and sunshine that was very nearly warm. Ashe's powerful Jaguar XJS ate up the miles, and Catrin sat back, relaxed, determined to enjoy the day, whatever Ashe's motives for visiting Liam. Because, no matter how much Ashe said he accepted that Liam wasn't his son, Catrin still wasn't totally convinced that he meant it.

When they arrived at the school Ashe parked the car in a row of vehicles full of waiting parents. Small boys came running from the building to greet their families, Liam among them, a head taller than most of his peers. He grinned from ear to ear as he saw Catrin with her companion, and beckoned them over.

'Hello, Cat. Gosh, it's you, Doctor. Hi. This is Mr Rowlands, my housemaster.'

'Good morning,' the young man said cheerfully. 'I sign them off as they leave and round them up when they come back.'

Catrin smiled. 'We've met before.'

Ashe shook hands with young Mr Rowlands. 'How do you do? My name's Hope-Ellison. I'm Catrin's fiancé.'

'Wow, are you?' said Liam, surprised.

Catrin, no less startled, accepted the young house-master's invitation to tea later, and gave Ashe a narrowed, speaking look as they took Liam off to the car.

'Ace!' He eyed it with enthusiasm. 'I bet this can move.'

'It can,' agreed Ashe, 'but not today. I don't think Catrin would approve if we were had up for speeding.'

Over the meal, in a hotel Julia had recommended for lunch, Liam got on with Ashe so well Catrin began to feel like an unwanted third, until Ashe halted Liam's account of his try in a rugby match the day before to suggest Catrin might not find the subject to her taste.

'You don't mind, do you, Cat?' demanded Liam in surprise.

'Of course not.' Catrin smiled at Ashe as they were served with roast turkey with all the trimmings. 'I was rather a fan in college. I shared a house in my third year with two members of the first fifteen.'

'Did you, indeed?' murmured Ashe, eyes gleaming.

'What position did they play?' demanded Liam.

'One was a tight head prop, the other played lock,' said Catrin, winning a look of deep respect from her brother as he helped himself to a vast quantity of roast potatoes. 'Broccoli too, and carrots,' she reminded him.

'You sound just like Mum,' he said, resigned. 'At least they don't have Brussels sprouts.' He shuddered graphically.

Ashe laughed, and admitted a similar dislike for the vegetable. 'It dates from my own schooldays.'

'Don't encourage him,' said Catrin, beginning on her lunch. 'Left to himself, Liam would exist on burgers, French fries and fizzy drinks.'

'They don't do burgers here,' said the boy with regret. 'Not on Sundays, anyway.'

'Which is why Mother recommended it, no doubt,' said Catrin, laughing. 'Eat that broccoli, or no pudding.' Not that the command was necessary. Liam was plainly enjoying himself so much he would have done anything she asked.

He told Ashe frankly that he'd been a bit worried when his mother had told him a friend was driving Catrin over for the day. 'I thought she meant Julian,' he said disparagingly, then brightened as the waitress presented him with a towering concoction of ice cream.

'You don't care for Julian?' asked Ashe casually, while Catrin poured coffee.

'He's all right.' Liam shrugged. 'Hasn't a clue about any kind of sport, though. I'm glad you're going to marry Dr Hope-Ellison instead, Cat.'

Catrin was speechless, and by the smile twitching the corner of Ashe's mouth he was well aware of it.

'Do you cut people up?' Liam asked him.

'No. I'm a physician. I treat the illnesses which don't require surgery.'

'Tell him about the camera on a tube,' said Catrin, resigned. 'He'll love it.'

She was right. Liam was utterly fascinated by the

whole process of endoscopy, and all the other more technical aspects of Ashe's work, and asked eager, intelligent questions for the remainder of their lunch.

Afterwards Ashe drove back to the school, where some of the younger fathers were passing a rugby ball round with their sons on one of the playing fields.

'It's too early for tea yet,' said Liam, and gave Ashe a diffident look. 'I don't suppose—'

'It's a long time since I played, but I used to be quite useful on the wing,' said Ashe, stripping off his jacket. He handed his watch to Catrin. 'Are you going to stay here, darling, or are you coming to watch?'

'I wouldn't miss it for the world,' she assured him, eyes glittering. 'I'm something of an authority on the game remember. The tight head prop I mentioned eventually played for Wales a couple of times.'

'Only twice?' said Ashe affably.

'He went off to work in America.'

'So did I. Remind me to tell you about it some time.'

Liam gave Catrin his blazer and tie, stripped off his sweater, and ran off with Ashe eagerly. Catrin sat on a bench and watched them. Their dark heads gleamed in the sun as Ashe did his best to prove he hadn't lost his skill. He passed and caught and kicked for touch, then watched with pride as Liam placed the ball upright on the ground, eyed the posts, then kicked the ball plumb between them, several feet above the crossbar. Eventually, just as Catrin was beginning to wish she'd brought a topcoat, they came jogging back to her, smiling and out of breath, but obviously highly pleased with themselves.

'Ashe must have been pretty good,' said Liam. 'He can still run quite fast.'

'Not as fast as you,' panted Ashe.

'A good thing it's dry. You're not too dirty for once,' said Catrin, interrupting the mutual admiration as she handed Liam his clothes. 'You'd both better dash off and wash before tea, though.'

'I'll show Ashe where to go,' said Liam.

'I told him to call me that,' said Ashe, interpreting her raised eyebrow.

'Come *on*,' urged Liam, 'or we'll be late. Mr Rowlands may smile a lot at you, Cat, but he'll wipe the floor with me.'

Catrin waved them off, deciding to sit in the car and make repairs to her face while she waited. She sighed. This had probably not been a good idea. Ashe, as was all too obvious, was plainly entranced with Liam. She didn't blame him. Liam did both his parents and the school credit.

As she left the car, a smiling young woman emerged from another nearby. 'Going in to tea?'

Catrin nodded, and, chatting pleasantly, they strolled back towards the building, where Liam came racing out, followed more slowly by Ashe.

'Goodness,' said Catrin's companion. 'Your son's the image of his father!'

CHAPTER TEN

CATRIN was very quiet on the way home, and Ashe gave up trying to talk after a while. When he suggested a meal in a pub *en route* Catrin agreed. They needed to talk, and a public place was probably the best place.

They arrived early at a small, quiet country pub, and had the bar to themselves. They took their drinks to a table tucked to one side of the inglenook, where a log fire blazed in welcome.

Ashe waited until she was seated, then looked at her challengingly. 'Well, Catrin?'

'Did you enjoy your day?' she countered, gazing into the flames.

'You know I did. It would have been hard not to in Liam's company. And yours.' He caught her eye. 'Though you enjoyed yourself less, I think.'

'Why did you introduce me as your fiancée?' she said, going into the attack.

Ashe frowned. 'Is *that* what was troubling you? Why? Isn't that what you are? When you brought up the subject of living together I assumed you meant you'd marry me sooner or later. I'd prefer sooner, Cat, but I'm doing my best not to rush you.'

'People don't get married to live together any more,' she pointed out.

'Catrin,' said Ashe, leaning across the table. 'I'm pushing forty. I want a home and if possible a family. Spending time with Liam has shown me how much I'm missing.'

'Have you given up the idea that he's your son?' she demanded.

Ashe straightened. 'I would be lying if I said that some small part of my brain won't give it up. But, even if he were, I know perfectly well there's nothing I could do. Nor would I wish to. He was chatting away about his mum and dad, not to mention his grandparents and an aunt called Hannah he seems very attached to. He's a great kid. I wouldn't turn his life upside down for the world.'

'But if you married me you would, of course, be related to him, however tenuously,' said Catrin without expression.

Ashe stared at her. 'You can't think that's anything to do with my wanting to marry you, Catrin? What sort of idiot do you think I am? I married last time for all the wrong reasons, remember. This time it's for love.' His eyes darkened. 'The love of my life.'

She gazed back, her throat thickening with sudden tears, and Ashe reached across the table and took her hand.

'The fact that Liam's not my son doesn't stop me from wanting a son—or a daughter—something like him. More than one, if we're lucky. And when it comes down to it, I suppose I'm conventional enough to want a wedding before a christening.'

Neither of them felt like eating, and after a while Ashe drove Catrin home.

'I'm not asking to come in tonight,' he said as they arrived. 'I've got a full day tomorrow, and I'm likely to finish late. So to avoid any of this rushing you object to I suggest we don't see each other for a day or two. I'll see you on Wednesday.'

Catrin felt oddly deflated. 'All right, Ashe. That's probably a good idea.' She gave him rather a wry little smile. 'Thank you for today. Liam had a great time.'

'Did Catrin?'

'Oh, yes,' she said, without hesitation. Every minute she spent with Ashe, whether arguing, making love, or just being together doing nothing, was infinitely preferable to any time spent without him. 'It was a lovely day, Ashe.'

He leaned close and kissed her gently. 'Go to bed early and get some sleep, sweetheart. You look tired.'

Catrin kissed him back lingeringly, and he tensed, his mouth suddenly urgent on hers, then he leapt out of the car and came round to open her door, shaking his head ruefully.

'Where you're concerned, darling, my control threshold is very low!'

She laughed, her wellbeing suddenly restored, and went inside, knowing he would wait until he saw her switch her light on in the flat.

Wednesday took a very long time to arrive. Catrin met up with Dinah for a meal and a film on Monday night, and went to a concert the night after, and each time came home to a message on her machine from Ashe.

'Is this a way of telling me you can manage very well without me?' he demanded, when she rang back late at night for the second evening running.

'No. I'm just doing the things I always did before I met up with you again,' she said, gratified to hear the note of displeasure in his voice. 'Barring Julian, of course.'

'Catrin,' he said quietly, 'I wouldn't ask you to change your life completely.'

'I know,' she assured him, not wishing to tell him that her social whirl was purely a means of making the time pass quickly until she saw him again.

When she did, Ashe was waiting for her, illegally parked as usual, on the double yellow lines outside the offices.

'Don't you ever get a ticket?' she said happily.

'I'm a doctor, remember!' He looked in the mirror. 'Who's the chap scowling at you back there?'

'One of my colleagues.'

'He looks like a puppy deprived of his bone.'

'He's got a very inconvenient crush on me.'

'Unreciprocated, I hope?'

'Too true. Quite apart from the fact that I don't find him in the least attractive, he's married.'

'Shall I discourage him for you?'

'If he saw you waiting for me I expect you already have,' Catrin assured him. 'What are we doing to-night?'

'Dinner at the Chesterton.'

'Very grand! I'll need to go home and change, then.'

Ashe drove her to the flat and took off his jacket, settling down to read the evening paper on her sofa while Catrin showered. There was an intimacy in the situation she found so appealing she could hardly wait for the time when Ashe reopened the subject of marriage. Part of her resistance had been objection to the way he'd sprung it on her at the school by announcing he was her fiancé. But, after thinking it over for the best part of three days, she found the idea of marriage and a family appealed to her strongly, as long as the man concerned was Ashe.

She did her face at top speed and hunted out the stockings she kept for special occasions, wishing her expensive cashmere dress hadn't come to grief in the fire. She put on last year's red wool shift, hopping from one foot to the other as she tried to do up the zip, but without success.

She went to the door. 'Ashe, could you do me up, please? My zip's stuck.'

He smiled and turned her away from him, his fingers cool against her back. After a while he said, 'It won't budge, sweetheart—up or down.'

'Just pull it apart, then, and I'll wear something else.'

Ashe tried to move the zip for a moment, then tugged hard, and the dress fell to the floor. Catrin stepped out of it and turned to face him, flushing as he stood motionless at the sight of her in a peach satin teddy and sheer stockings.

'What are you trying to do to me?' he asked huskily, and closed the space between them, crushing her against him.

'I wasn't trying to do anything!' she gasped.

'You don't have to try.' He ran his hands down her silk-covered spine, shaping her against his taut body, then he lifted her against him suddenly, kissing her as though he meant to devour her, his tongue seeking out the contours of her open mouth. Catrin's knees buckled as he thrust aside satin straps and bared her to the waist. She made little choking sounds as his mouth and fingertips wrought delicious agony she could hardly bear, and she clasped her hand behind his head to hold him closer, and exulted as she felt a great shudder run through him. She collapsed on the bed, pulling him with her, all thoughts of dinner and everything else forgotten as he tore off his clothes and she helped him feverishly, both of them lost to everything but the consuming desire for the union which fused them together at last, body and soul.

The last throes of their passion had barely receded when Ashe shot up, staring down into her dazed face in remorse.

'Catrin, I'm *sorry*!'

There was no need for him to explain. She bit her lip and gave him a crooked little smile. 'Just as well I was going to say yes tonight, in the circumstances.'

His eyes glittered in triumph. 'Do you mean that?'

'Anyway, it was my fault as much as yours.' She pulled a wry little face. 'I was a bit shameless, wasn't I?'

'Have you any idea what it does to a man to know the woman in his arms wants him so much, my darling?' Ashe stretched out beside her and drew her into his arms, one leg over hers in an attitude of such intimate possession her stomach muscles contracted. 'Did you mean that you'd decided marriage was a good idea?'

'With you, yes.' Catrin buried her face in his shoulder. 'I quite like the idea of a family, too,' she added in a muffled voice.

'Since you drove me out of my mind to the point where I forgot to prevent one, it's just as well,' he said, a note of such undisguised male satisfaction in his voice that she kicked him with a bare foot. 'Not,' he added, 'that one swallow necessarily makes a summer. I might have to persevere for some time before the desired result.'

'Good,' said Catrin. 'I like it when you—persevere.'

'If you talk like that we'll never get that dinner,' he said sternly, one hand caressing her hip.

She looked up, her eyes heavy with a look which brought a sharp intake of breath from Ashe. 'Do we have to go out?' she whispered. 'Are you averse to scrambled eggs? Later?'

'Much later,' he agreed hoarsely. 'Anything you say. Or want. Or need. Always, my darling. God, Catrin, I love you so much.'

Catrin rang her mother next day to confirm that Julia and Richard were recovered enough for Sunday lunch the following weekend. 'I'm bringing a friend, remember,' she warned.

'But he's not a friend exactly, is he, Catrin?' Julia's voice was dry. 'I received the obligatory letter from my son this morning. French is obviously not Liam's star subject, but even with his bizarre spelling I gather that your companion was your fiancé.'

'That's how Ashe introduced himself to Liam's housemaster, certainly. Up to that point the relationship was less well defined, which is why I haven't mentioned it sooner. One of the reasons for our visit on Sunday is to ask your blessing.'

'But that's wonderful! If you love him I'll be happy to give my blessing, darling.' Julia paused. 'Liam's letter was as brief as he could get away with, as usual, but he mentioned the name Ashe more than once. Didn't you know someone called Ashe years ago, in Pembrokeshire?'

'Yes, Mother. Ashe with an "e". It's the same one. He's the doctor I met again in hospital after the fire. Until then I hadn't seen him for ten years.'

'A rekindled flame, then,' said Julia thoughtfully.

'Very much so,' said Catrin, her heart thumping at the thought of the night before.

'I can't wait to meet him. He seems to have made quite an impression on Liam. Richard and I were already booked for lunchtime drinks on Sunday, I'm afraid, so warn Ashe that the meal will be a bit late. If we're not there when you arrive let yourself in.'

Catrin spent the intervening time in a state of euphoria that was hard to conceal from anyone, least of all Dinah, when Catrin went rushing upstairs on the Sunday morning to show her the ring Ashe had bought her the day before.

'How absolutely lovely,' said Dinah, examining the solitaire emerald. 'I'm impressed. Bring him up for a drink some time. I must tell the good doctor how lucky he is.'

'We're both lucky. We've been given a second chance,' said Catrin simply, admiring her ring. 'Next week we're going house-hunting.'

'So when's the happy day?'

'Soon,' said Catrin, colouring.

'What I'd give to be able to blush like that,' said Dinah, shaking her head. 'So the bridegroom's impatient, is he? And who can blame him?'

'I'm impatient too,' said Catrin honestly. 'Ashe and I have a lot of time to make up.'

Due to the ruin of her red dress Catrin had visited the dress department of the local store where Dinah worked for something new in one of her lunch hours, feeling the occasion warranted it. With Dinah urging her on she'd spent rather more than intended on a dress as simple as a sweater in her favourite shade of leaf-green.

Ashe approved, strongly, when he came to collect her. 'You look like spring,' he said, kissing her.

'It's my second dress more or less like this since Christmas,' she told him as they went down the stairs. She gestured at the pineapple. 'That caused the concussion, I think, but the fire put paid to the dress. It was ruined.'

'At least you're wearing less frivolous shoes today,' remarked Ashe, glancing at her feet. 'Didn't you tell me something about four-inch heels?'

'Never again!' she assured him as she slid into the car. 'From now on Catrin will be the soul of propriety.'

'I hope not!' Ashe switched on the ignition and gave her a look which curled her toes. 'I like the Catrin of the past few nights. Not much propriety then, my lovely little wanton.'

'Really, Doctor,' she said primly, 'I'd rather you didn't say such things while you're driving.'

'When, then?' he demanded.

'Tonight, maybe?'

'No maybe about it!'

They were heading for the outskirts of a village near Stratford-upon-Avon, where Julia and Richard Harper lived in a large converted cottage situated in two acres of wild garden.

'Richard keeps it wild on purpose, so Liam can play in it,' said Catrin as Ashe parked the car.

The cottage, which had pink-washed walls and small windows, gave out an air of welcome Ashe admired instantly.

'I envy them the house!'

'Lovely, isn't it? We're to let ourselves in because Mother and Richard are at a drinks party on the other side of the village. Follow me.' Catrin unlocked the door and ushered Ashe into a hall where a beamed low ceiling and uneven wood floor exuded a charm peculiarly its own.

'This is the sort of thing I'd like myself,' he said, looking round.

'Only if you have a playroom where someone like Liam can do his own thing.'

'With luck we will have,' he said quietly, and took her in his arms and kissed her.

Catrin smiled radiantly. 'Come on, let's go into the garden. I love it when the daffodils are in bloom.'

'How lyrical!' he said, following her along the corridor to the back door.

'I feel lyrical, Ashe,' she said seriously, and reached up and kissed him. 'I give you three guesses why.'

'I don't need three guesses, darling. I feel the same.'

They went down the paved path, past flowerbeds where spring flowers were pushing their heads up amongst the bushy perennials, and on towards a flat stretch near the far hedge, where Richard had mowed an almost full-size wicket for his son to practise his cricket skills.

They wandered round the large, untidy garden, enjoying the cold-edged sunshine, until the sound of an approaching car sent them back into the house to meet Julia as she hurried in through the front door, arms outstretched to hug her daughter.

'Hello, darling, sorry we're a bit late.' She released Catrin, holding her hand out with a smile to Ashe. 'Welcome, Dr Hope-Ellison. I'm Julia Harper.'

Ashe took the hand in his, smiling warmly. 'How do you do? I'd rather you called me Ashe.'

'Then I will.' Julia took off her scarf and smoothed a few stray strands up into her coiled hair, calling out to her husband, 'Come on, Richard, get a move on. These two must be dying of thirst.'

Catrin reached up to kiss her stepfather's cheek, then stood back with a smile. 'Dr Richard Harper, meet Dr Hope-Ellison.'

Richard grinned, holding out a large hand, and Catrin caught her mother's approving eye as the two tall, dark men shook hands, Richard genial and welcoming, Ashe more reserved. Then Catrin held out her left hand to her mother, and there were exclamations over her ring and eager questions about the wedding.

'We haven't decided yet,' said Catrin, looking at Ashe. 'It's all happened rather suddenly.'

'I'm leaving it to Catrin to name the day,' he said smoothly, and Julia reminded her husband that no one had a drink, then left the men together to talk shop as she took her daughter into the kitchen.

'Won't be long, love. There's a roast sitting in the warming oven. Sorry we had to be out, but it was a do for the Children's Society, and as I'm secretary we had to be there.' Julia thrust various vegetables on to cook, then turned to Catrin. 'But never mind that. Your Ashe is rather gorgeous, Catrin. *And*,' she added, 'older than I expected. He couldn't have been a mere boy all those years ago, slyboots.'

'No,' said Catrin, stirring gravy. 'Back then I was afraid you wouldn't let me go on seeing him if you knew he was so much older than me.'

'Not only older, darling,' said Julia dryly. 'Ashe is a very attractive man the way he is, but ten years ago he must have bowled you over.'

'Dinah said that, too.' Catrin grinned. 'Anyway, that was then and this is now, so tell me you approve, Mother.'

'Of course I do, darling.' Julia hugged her close. 'I was beginning to think you had no intention of marrying anyone, just like my independent sister. And I really quite fancy some grandchildren some time, you know.'

'You look too young to be a grandmother!'

'Thank you kindly. Now let's get this lot on the table and feed those men.'

Because Julia and Richard were excellent hosts, and Ashe a very appreciative guest, the lunch was a success. Catrin watched him as he praised the food and expressed his admiration of the house, entertaining the Harpers with an account of his fun on the school playing field with their son the week before. But Catrin was deeply uneasy. Ashe was putting on a performance, and behind the charm and bonhomie something was so horribly wrong she was sick with worry by the time they left.

Catrin was glad to get away at last. Another hour of Ashe's faultless performance and she would have been ready to scream.

The moment they were in the car the curtain came down on Ashe's act. He drove the first few miles in complete silence, and when Catrin eventually asked if he'd enjoyed the day he said, 'Of course. Your mother's utterly charming. She looks years younger than her age. Your stepfather, too,' he added pointedly.

'Your stepfather', not Richard, she thought, and eyed him apprehensively. 'What's wrong, Ashe?'

'Why should something be wrong?' he said lightly. 'I thought I behaved very well.'

'Oh, you did,' she assured him. 'Quite the star turn. I almost applauded.'

'I'd rather not discuss it now,' he said curtly. 'We're running into fog.'

When they arrived at Orchard House Ashe followed Catrin upstairs, his silence beginning to stretch her nerves to breaking point. When she unlocked the door she went straight through to the kitchen to make coffee, telling Ashe to pour himself a drink.

'No, thanks,' he said, leaning in the kitchen doorway. 'I'd prefer coffee.'

'And I'd like some explanations,' said Catrin eventually. She handed a beaker to him, then went to curl up in the corner of her sofa. Ashe, instead of joining her on the sofa as usual, took the armchair opposite, his eyes speculative.

'So that's your stepfather,' he said at last.

Catrin's eyes narrowed. 'And you obviously took an instant dislike to him, though for the life of me I can't see why.'

'I'd seen him before,' he said, and drank some of the coffee.

'I know that! You caught a glimpse of him when he drove me back that night.'

'I wasn't thinking straight that night.'

'You mean you'd had one brandy too many.'

He nodded his head gravely. 'Whichever. Anyway, I thought he looked familiar, but I only had a glimpse and couldn't place him. If I'd known he was a doctor I might have thought we'd met professionally.'

'Hardly,' said Catrin coldly. 'Richard's just a general practitioner, not a lordly consultant like you.'

'I don't think I deserve that,' he returned, his eyes hardening.

She shrugged. 'Possibly not. I'm angry because you spoiled my day, I suppose.' She twisted the ring on her finger. 'It rather takes the shine out of all this.'

'I'd actually seen Dr Harper before,' Ashe informed her once more, his eyes on the glittering emerald as she toyed with it.

Catrin looked at him, frowning. 'Where?'

'He was the man I saw making love to you in the car ten years ago.' He breathed in deeply. 'He raised his head for an instant, and I saw his face above your hair before I took to my heels. I've never forgotten it.'

She looked at him in horror. 'You mean it was *Richard* you saw making love to someone that day?'

'Not to someone, Catrin. To you.'

Catrin sprang to her feet, standing over him, and Ashe rose slowly until she was forced to look up into his face.

'It wasn't *me*!' she said passionately. 'I can't believe it was Richard, either. But it definitely wasn't me.' She waited, but Ashe's face remained cold, withdrawn. 'You still don't believe me.' She turned away, but he caught her by the shoulders and turned her back to face him.

'Up until today I believed you because I wanted to. But after meeting Richard Harper face to face—'

'You decided it was me, after all, indulging in a little hanky-panky with my stepfather in broad daylight all those years ago,' Catrin said dully, and moved out of his hold. 'Only he wasn't my stepfather then.'

'Which makes it marginally better, I suppose,' said Ashe grimly.

'Who for?'

'Your mother?'

Catrin looked at him in silence for a moment, then slowly, feeling as though she were removing part of herself, she took off the ring and held it out. 'I think you'd better have this back, Ashe. You've obviously never believed me from the start. I couldn't convince you about Liam, and I can't get it through your head that I didn't go straight from your arms into Richard's that day, either.'

'I know I'm not Liam's father,' said Ashe, ignoring the ring. 'After meeting Harper today it's pretty obvious Liam's his son. A son any man would be proud of. It was wishful thinking to hope he was mine, but not entirely illogical after what happened between you and me ten years ago, Catrin.'

'What I find illogical,' she said bitterly, 'is that you still think Richard and I were having fun and games behind my mother's back.' She sought for the cruellest thing she could think of to hurt him, and raised contemptuous eyes to his. 'Sex is so good with you, Ashe, I don't suppose I'll ever find anyone so compatible. But without trust what's the good of that? If you behave like this over something you believe happened years ago, how would you be in the future? Ready to punch the postman if I smiled at him? Or wonder where I was if I were half an hour late coming home? Or even doubt the provenance of any children we might have?'

By this time Ashe was very pale, his face haggard as he stared at the ring she was still holding out. 'If you give this back to me, Catrin, I'll keep it. I didn't give it lightly.'

'No,' she agreed. 'Nor am I giving it back lightly, either. I didn't believe you could hurt me more than you did all those years ago, but I was wrong. And I refuse to subject myself to any more of it. Please take your ring and your grubby little suspicions and go. Now.'

Ashe looked at the ring, cleared his throat as though he were about to speak, then shrugged, a look of icy indifference on his face, and walked out of the room, closing the door very quietly, just as he'd done once before. Only this time, instead of running after him, Catrin bolted it behind him, then took the ring into the bedroom, fetched its box and stuffed it into a padded envelope. She wrote Ashe's full title on it, added the address, and left it ready to post the next day. Then, knowing it would be harder to do the longer she left it, she rang her mother to say she'd arrived safely, but the engagement was off.

'Darling, no!' said Julia, horrified. There was silence on the line for a moment, then she said carefully. 'Am I allowed to ask why?'

'Ten years was too long a gap to bridge after all,' said Catrin, fighting to keep her voice steady.

'Was it something *we* did?' Julia sounded close to tears.

'Absolutely not, Mother. This is down to Ashe and me. That rekindled flame you once mentioned just sort of died, after all.'

'I can't believe this. You seemed so happy today. Catrin, tell me the truth. Are you *sure* we didn't upset Ashe in some way?'

'Very sure. It was Ashe who upset me.' Catrin swallowed hard. 'Look, Mother, I must go. I'll talk to you tomorrow.'

CHAPTER ELEVEN

ONCE Catrin made it generally known the engagement was off, she settled down grimly to the task of getting over Ashe for the second time. Only now there was so much more to get over. Last time she had never really expected it to be more than just a holiday romance. This time, for a brief, ecstatic period, she had finally begun to believe it would last forever.

Dinah, as always, was a source of constant support and comfort.

'A terrible pity,' she said to Catrin, that first Monday evening, 'but it's not the end of the world. You know that, of course, because you've been through all this before. But this time it's worse, isn't it?'

Catrin nodded, swallowing the lump that seemed permanently lodged in her throat. 'Last time I had a change of scene to help. I went to college. This time I'll just have to bite the bullet and soldier on as best I can.'

'Good girl,' approved Dinah. 'Look round for someone else. That usually does the trick.'

'Yes,' said Catrin thoughtfully. 'Good idea.'

She didn't have to look far. She rang Julian next day, and for once he was at his desk in Pennington, instead of on his travels. When she told him that Ashe was no longer part of her life, Julian promptly asked her out for a meal the following Friday.

Catrin did her best to put Ashe and his accusations from her mind, but she missed him badly, and cursed herself for ever having made love with him in her bed. By day she had her work to occupy her mind, and in the evenings she made sure there was no time to dwell on Ashe, but at night he wouldn't stay banished. She tossed and turned in her lonely bed, horrified to find that she yearned for his physical presence, longed for the touch of his lips and hands, and the breathtaking demands of his body.

But this would pass, she told herself fiercely, when she wandered round the flat in the small hours, trying to make herself tired enough to sleep.

To speed her recovery programme Catrin enrolled at a gym, and three nights a week worked hard there to channel off excess energy, but, though her shape improved, her heart stubbornly refused to mend.

Its healing process was further impeded when she came out of the office one night to find a familiar car parked at the kerb. Her heart skipped a beat, she hesitated, then walked past the Jaguar, resolutely ignoring the occupant as she made for Julian's car, which was parked in a more legal spot a few yards away. Catrin smiled brightly as Julian jumped out to greet her, and she ducked into his car, her heart beating so hard she thought he must be able to hear it as the sleek shape of the Jaguar cruised past, with Ashe at the wheel.

Luckily Julian was taking her to a cinema. She was able to recover somewhat during the film, though afterwards she had no idea what it was about, and had to busk it when Julian discussed it afterwards over supper in his favourite Greek restaurant.

When Catrin got home she felt exhausted, as though she'd run a marathon, and when she checked her messages felt reluctant to play them back.

'Catrin,' said Ashe's familiar deep tones. 'I want to see you. I have something to discuss, so ring me to arrange a meeting. As soon as possible, please.'

Catrin slumped on the sofa, still in her topcoat, staring at her shoes. She wanted to ring him so much it took sheer strength of will to stay where she was and think it over. Then she got up and played the message back, her eyes narrowing as this time she took in the peremptory tone of his message.

No! She definitely would not ring him. There was nothing conciliatory about Ashe's request. Did he think she would just drop everything and run the minute he crooked his little finger? Presumably that was why he'd been waiting when she finished work this evening, taking it for granted that she'd fall in with his wishes. Yet that night, contrary to expectations, Catrin slept all night, without waking once to pace the floor.

Catrin left early next morning for the Harper household, ready by this time to answer the questions she knew Julia must be wanting to ask. But neither Julia nor Richard said much, other than to enquire after her health, and it was only when Richard was called out to a patient later that Julia brought the subject up.

'What really happened, Catrin?' she asked.

Catrin thought of prevaricating, of saying vague things about incompatibility, but in the end she told her mother the whole story, which, to make sense, had to include her first encounter with Ashe. The only thing Catrin left out was the identity of the man Ashe had seen in the car ten years before.

'So. If Ashe thought Liam was his son, he must have been your lover,' said Julia thoughtfully, eyeing her daughter. 'Your first, at that.'

Catrin nodded, flushing. 'And the only one for some time, believe me.'

'You mean you couldn't bear the thought of anyone else in that way after Ashe?'

'Right. But this time I'm not going to be so silly. I've started going out with Julian again,' she added defiantly.

Her mother, who did not care for Julian, made no comment. 'Have you seen Ashe since?'

Catrin described the incident of the night before. 'He left a message on my machine last night, telling me to ring him.'

'And did you?'

'Not on your life! I don't take kindly to orders, from Ashe or any other man.' She jumped up. 'Fancy a walk before dinner?'

When Catrin returned to Pennington on the Sunday evening there was another message from Ashe, in much the same vein as the first, but she clung to her pride and refused to let herself yield to curiosity, or to temptation.

But it was with a feeling of inevitability that Catrin

emerged late from the office the following evening to find the Jaguar at the kerb, and Ashe himself waiting at the door for her.

'Good evening,' he said politely.

Catrin couldn't bring herself to return the courtesy. 'What do you want, Ashe? I'm tired and I want to get home.'

'Then I'll drive you there.'

'No, thanks.'

Ashe gave a glance up and down the street. 'We can hardly talk here.'

'I don't want to talk anywhere!'

'But I do. It won't take long. Once we get to your place you're free to go.'

Catrin looked up at his set face, rather glad to find he looked even more haggard than she did. 'Very well,' she said distantly.

They were on their way through the pouring rain before Ashe spoke. 'How are you?'

'Fine.'

'You didn't return my messages.'

'I didn't see the point.'

'Without speaking to me it's unlikely you would.'

Catrin's temper was beginning to rise, but she bit back the words she longed to hurl at him. By the time they arrived at Orchard House she had herself well in hand.

'May I come up?' he asked.

'I'd rather you didn't,' she said coldly. 'Say what you have to say here.'

'Very well.' His voice was equally cold. 'I should

have acknowledged your return of the ring, but thought it as well to leave speaking to you until now, when sufficient time had elapsed.'

Time for what? she wondered.

'You must know what I'm about to ask,' he said, staring through the windscreen.

'I'm afraid not.'

He breathed in deeply, then turned his eyes on her profile. 'By now you must know whether you're pregnant or not.'

'Oh, that,' she said indifferently, and his hand caught hers in a bruising grip.

'Are you?' he demanded.

Catrin turned without hurry to meet his eyes. 'Pregnant, Ashe? Why should I tell you? On past showing you'd never be able to believe the child was yours!'

He winced, then released her hand and stared ahead again. 'Nevertheless, I need to know.'

Catrin undid the seat belt, amazed she felt so calm. 'Sorry, Ashe. I'm nothing to do with you any more.'

'If you're expecting my child you most certainly are. I have a right to know, Catrin.'

'You will know some time, no doubt,' she assured him. 'Is the maternity ward at the General good?'

Ashe turned on her and brought her face round to his. 'Stop playing with me, Catrin. You've had your fun. Now tell me the truth.'

'Why? You've never believed any of it up to now,' she snapped, and pushed him away. 'Goodbye, Ashe.' She slid from the car and ran up the steps to Orchard House without a backward glance.

Inside the flat she was annoyed to find she was trembling, and made for the phone.

'Dinah? Can I come up, please? I've got a suggestion to make.'

Next day Catrin asked George Duffield to spare her a few minutes, and told him she'd like to take part of her annual holiday as soon as possible.

'Certainly, my dear,' he said promptly. 'My wife gave me a lecture for letting you come back too soon after your adventures in the fire. You look tired. Find a place in the sun somewhere, Catrin, and come back full of energy for the new financial year!'

She smiled gratefully, and a week later she was on her way to the West Indies with Dinah, to a hotel in St Lucia where their rooms opened directly onto the beach. The price of the holiday paid for everything, right down to the last banana cocktail, and there was nothing to do other than sunbathe, swim, eat the delicious food—and get over Ashe.

'This is wonderful,' she told Dinah when they arrived. 'No columns of figures, no rain, no frost, no men lurking to ambush me or leave messages on my phone.' She sighed. 'Heaven!'

Dinah agreed contentedly. 'Here's to Harry,' she said, raising her glass. 'I used to lecture him about his gambling, but now I'm basking in the rewards of his luck at the Cheltenham Gold Cup.'

'What was the horse's name?' asked Catrin, pleased to find she could actually laugh again.

Laughter had been missing in her life since she'd returned the ring to Ashe.

'Horses—very much in the plural, dear. When I applied to Harry for a sub for my hols, he produced a wad of notes, the darling man.'

'Didn't he want to come with you?'

'Of course he did. Next time, I promised him. I say, Cat, dear, do you think that tall, distinguished man over there is on his own?'

Catrin returned to Pennington feeling rested and fit to deal with anything. She rang her mother as soon as she got in, described the holiday in glowing terms, asked after Liam and Richard, then frowned as she heard Ashe had been in contact with Julia.

'I was prepared for that, of course,' said Julia. 'I told him you'd gone away on holiday with a friend.'

'You didn't tell him which one, I hope!'

'No. I followed your instructions to the letter.'

'I never really thought he'd get in touch with you, though. I hope he didn't upset you, Mother?'

'Not in the least. He was very polite. Has he left any more messages on your phone?'

'I switched it off while I was away.'

'You don't intend to relent, then?'

'No. It's over, Mother. I'll see you on Saturday. Give my love to Richard.'

Although Catrin duly switched on her answering machine, there were no messages from Ashe on it during the next few days. Life was oddly peaceful. Julian was away on one of his foraging expeditions, Dinah had taken an extra week's holiday and gone to Cornwall to visit her parents, and the ground-floor flat was still not ready for habitation. Catrin had Orchard House to herself for a while. This was no problem, since she spent very little time at home other than to sleep.

There were two snags in her determinedly serene routine. One was the constant expectation of seeing Ashe, or hearing from him in one way or another. The other was Graham Parrish, the married Lothario who'd always been a thorn in Catrin's flesh. He announced to all concerned that he was getting a divorce, and, though this was of no interest whatsoever to Catrin, the soon-to-be free Graham promptly began to make overtures he assumed she'd welcome.

The man became so irritating that Catrin grew desperate to know how to discourage him. The answer came one evening, when, as usual since her return from St Lucia, he was by her side when she finished work, telling her that soon he'd be free to take her out for a meal or to the theatre, or whatever she wanted. Catrin was seriously thinking of hitting him with her briefcase when a familiar voice said, 'Is this man annoying you, Catrin?'

She looked up into Ashe's face, forgetting for the moment she'd never intended speaking to him again. 'Ashe—hello. Have you met Graham Parrish?'

'I don't think I have,' said Ashe, subjecting the man to one of his annihilating blue stares. 'How do you do? My name's Hope-Ellison.'

Catrin watched, fascinated, as her importuning colleague seemed to shrivel. He uttered a few disjointed words in acknowledgement and took himself off.

'Thank you,' said Catrin with sincere gratitude. 'He's about to be divorced, and is under the false impression I'm pleased about it.'

'If he made you glad to see me I'm grateful to him,' said Ashe dryly. 'May I drive you home, or were you bound somewhere else?'

'No. Thank you. A lift home would be nice. I've had a hard day.'

'So have I.' He held the car door for her, then got in and looked at her for a moment before switching on the ignition. 'You look very brown and healthy, Catrin. You obviously enjoyed your holiday.'

'It was wonderful.'

'Was Fellowes the friend you went with?' he asked casually.

'No. I went with Dinah Martin. My friend from the flat upstairs.'

'When she didn't answer her phone, I hoped your companion was Mrs Martin.'

Catrin stared at him. 'You rang Dinah?'

'When I couldn't reach you I was anxious.' His mouth twisted. 'Strange as it may seem to you, Catrin, I care about your welfare.'

Her holiday had restored Catrin's sense of proportion. She was no longer filled with a desire for revenge. 'You needn't worry any more, Ashe. I'm not pregnant. I knew that last time we met. But I wanted to hurt you.'

'And I provided you with the best weapon possible to do it,' he said grimly. 'Why are you admitting it now? I could have gone on suffering far longer than this.'

'Because I've recovered my equilibrium.' She gave him a sidelong look. 'Up to the time we last met my emotions had see-sawed rather violently, one way and another. I'm back to normal now.'

'How very nice for you,' he said with sarcasm. 'I wish I could say the same. Despite my seniority over you, Catrin, I seem to be less in control of my emotions.'

'Well, at least you can stop worrying over whether I'm pregnant or not,' she said consolingly.

'Don't patronise me, dammit,' he snarled, and parked the car outside Orchard House. 'Couldn't you tell I was *hoping* you were pregnant? That it seemed the only way to get you back?'

Catrin stared blindly at the familiar street, hating Ashe for disturbing her hard-won acceptance of life without him. 'Why should it have done that?' she snapped. 'What makes you think I'd have acknowledged you as the father even if I had been expecting a baby?'

Ashe sat like a man turned to stone. 'You mean you'd have brought up our child in ignorance of my identity.'

It was a statement, not a question, and she thawed slightly. 'I don't know. Because it didn't arise. Thank you for bringing me home.' She smiled crookedly. 'And for frightening off my persistent Romeo.'

'My pleasure,' he said dryly, and raised her hand to his lips for an instant. 'Goodbye, Catrin. Take good care of yourself. I shan't bother you again.'

Catrin got out of the car and went indoors filled with such a deep sense of dismay she felt ill. Ashe's parting words had been very final. Which, of course, was what she'd wanted. He'd finally achieved acceptance. Perfect. And now she felt as though her world had ended. Again.

Her first instinct was to run for home and the comfort of her mother's arms, but Catrin refused to allow herself that weakness. Instead she rang Julia and asked if she could postpone coming down until the following weekend. By then she would be back on an even keel again, she promised herself. This weekend she would tough it out alone.

But in the end she wasn't obliged to make the struggle, since Julian rang and asked her out to dinner. She was grateful. Other nights she could manage. But Saturday night was hard to bear alone under the circumstances.

To Catrin's surprise Julian took her to the Chesterton. Her heart contracted as she remembered the only other occasion she'd been asked to dine at the hotel's famed restaurant. Ashe had taken her to bed instead, the memory of it so vivid her heart gave a violent leap in her chest at the thought of it.

'Is it a special occasion?' she asked, as they were shown to a table.

'It is rather,' said Julian, holding a chair for her. 'I've done pretty well with my sales figures. A hefty bonus came my way, so I thought we'd celebrate.' He insisted on ordering the most expensive dishes on the menu, with wine to match, and Catrin did her very best to enjoy the evening.

From Julian's point of view she was obviously succeeding, since he grew expansive over coffee, telling her how glad he was that she'd decided not to marry her doctor after all.

'He's a consultant,' she said automatically.

'Whatever!' Julian dismissed it impatiently, then hesitated, making patterns on the cloth with his coffee spoon. 'Anyway, what I'm trying to say, Catrin, is I thought you and I might make a go of it instead.'

But Catrin wasn't listening. She was staring past him, her eyes on the tall, familiar figure arriving at a table on the far side of the room. Ashe was not alone. The woman with him was blonde, smartly dressed, somewhere in her late thirties, and, worst of all, the pair were so deep in conversation this was obviously not the first evening they'd spent together.

'I've given you a shock,' said Julian indulgently. 'I know I've always been wary of commitment, preferred playing the field and so on, but when you got engaged to Hope-Ellison I was pretty shattered. Catrin,' he added sharply, 'are you listening?'

She turned dazed, uncomprehending eyes on Julian's face. 'I'm sorry. What were you saying?'

He looked at her ruefully for a moment, then sighed. 'Nothing important.' He downed the rest of his wine. 'I'm away next week, so I shan't see you for a while.'

'Ring me when you get back,' said Catrin, pulling herself together. 'I'll cook a meal for you for a change.'

She was glad the meal was over, suddenly in a hurry to leave the restaurant before Ashe could notice her. When Julian drove her home she thanked him, but asked him would he mind if she didn't ask him up for a coffee.

'Sorry to be so feeble. I suddenly feel very tired. I need to get to bed.'

'You mean you saw Hope-Ellison with a blonde and you're jealous as hell,' contradicted Julian. 'Did you think I didn't notice?'

Catrin gave a strangled sob, then shot a horrified look of apology at him as the tears she'd been holding back for weeks began pouring down her face.

Julian stared at her, aghast, then reached into the glove compartment and handed her a box of tissues. 'I think you'd better let me come up and *I'll* make the coffee,' he said after a while, when the storm showed no signs of abating. 'I can't leave you like this, Catrin.'

She nodded blindly, and Julian hurried her into Orchard House and up to her flat, where he pushed her down on the sofa and went off to the kitchen to fill the kettle.

'I didn't know I was so noble,' he said bitterly, when he handed her a steaming mug later.

'I'm so sorry, Julian,' she said thickly, blowing her nose. 'I haven't cried since Ashe and I broke up. I don't know why I chose tonight to emote all over you.'

'You didn't choose,' he said, resigned. 'The sight of the suave doctor with another woman obviously unlocked the floodgates.'

Julian was remarkably kind under the circumstances, and after he'd gone Catrin felt utterly wretched, full of remorse for spoiling his evening. But far worse was her self-disgust at the jealousy torturing her.

Ashe hadn't been long in finding someone else, she thought viciously. While not so long ago he'd told little gullible Catrin she was the love of his life. Perhaps that was his line to all the women he charmed into bed. At the thought of Ashe in bed with the blonde she began to pace round the flat like an angry tigress, her swollen eyes glittering with rage all the more hard to bear because it was unwarranted. She had sent Ashe away. Somehow it had never occurred to her that he'd go straight to the arms of another woman.

You were with Julian, said a voice in her mind, and Catrin shrugged impatiently. That was different. She had no desire at all to go to bed with Julian. Not, she realised, probing the wound, that the thought of Ashe in bed with the blonde hurt most. It was the way they'd been so engrossed in conversation, so very obviously interested in each other. In the way she had once believed exclusive to her own relationship with Ashe.

CHAPTER TWELVE

WHEN Catrin arrived at the cottage the following Friday evening, Julia was shocked at the sight of her daughter. 'Darling, you look terrible. Are you ill?'

'Careful, Julia,' said Richard, dumping down a suitcase. 'She practically bit my head off when I tried to take her pulse.'

'Sorry,' said Catrin, kissing her mother. 'I'm just tired. I haven't been sleeping well lately.'

'Nor eating,' said Julia, frowning. 'Right. Good food, nice fresh country air, and early nights for you, my girl. If you can't sleep you can have my radio and listen to books on tape until you drop off. Better than sleeping pills.'

'You should prescribe them to your patients,' said Catrin, smiling at her large stepfather. 'How's Liam?'

After a week of trying to recover from the shock of Ashe with a new woman, Catrin was not averse to a little spoiling from her mother and Richard. All week she had put in as much overtime as possible, and worked out at the gym on the other evenings. But the nights had been agony. And after six nights with only an hour or so of sleep apiece Catrin knew very well she looked far from her best.

'No chance of getting back with Ashe, then,' said

Julia, when she followed Catrin up to the pretty little room always kept ready for her.

'I saw him dining with a very attractive blonde last Saturday.' Catrin unzipped her holdall. 'So that's that.'

Julia looked unconvinced. 'Blonde or no blonde, you still love him madly, I think.'

'"Madly" being the operative word.' Catrin rounded on her mother. 'I've always thought jealousy was such an unnecessary, degrading sort of emotion. One I would never stoop to! Now I know better. One look at Ashe last Saturday and I could have murdered him—*and* the blonde.' She ran a hand through her hair distractedly. 'I was so jealous I felt sick. Still do. All week that's all I've been able to think of. I've been working on auto-pilot.'

'But you still love him.'

'Oh, yes,' said Catrin wearily. 'I still love him. And the joke is, Mother, I have a really nasty feeling I always will.'

After twenty-four hours of life in the Harper household, Catrin looked very little better. She'd borrowed Julia's radio, as bidden, and, though it was comforting to have someone read to her, she was a couple of hours into Jane Austen's *Mansfield Park* before she finally fell asleep that first night, and earned much censure from her mother next morning because half a slice of toast was all she could manage for breakfast.

Later she obediently went shopping with Julia, and came back from Stratford with a new sweater and two cancellations for *As You Like It* at the Royal Shakespeare Theatre in which one of Julia's favourite television actors was playing one of the major roles. Richard was on call, and therefore unable to join them.

'Much to my sorrow,' he lied cheerfully, and looked at Catrin with a professional eye. 'You still look very peaky, love.'

'I know,' she said dispiritedly.

'We did some shopping,' said Julia, changing the subject, and held a sweater up in front of her. 'Do you like this? Catrin bought one too.'

They went down to the Fox and Hounds in the village for a pub lunch, and as the sun came out in the afternoon Julia and Catrin went for a walk, leaving Richard to watch racing on the television with his phone at his elbow.

That night, after the determinedly busy day, and the evening at the theatre, Catrin listened to less of *Mansfield Park* before she fell asleep, and woke next morning feeling marginally better.

'You don't look it, though,' she told her reflection, and stood under the shower, shampooing her hair vigorously, and went down to breakfast with it swathed in a towel.

The morning was spent in preparation for lunch. Catrin eyed the vast leg of lamb in dismay. 'All that for us?'

'I make the leftovers into shepherd's pies and put them in the freezer ready for Liam's holidays,' said Julia, chopping carrots. She smiled at Catrin. 'Let's give Richard a treat and put our new sweaters on for lunch. I like that shade on you; it's the exact violet-blue of Canterbury bells.'

'Matches the circles under my eyes,' said Catrin prosaically.

'And leave your hair loose, darling—oh, bother, there's the phone again. That means Richard will have to dash off.'

'I hope you get back to eat some of this food,' said Catrin, as Richard came in to say he was called out.

'Don't worry. Our new trainee takes over at mid-day. I'm not passing up my Sunday lunch, believe me,' he assured her, and kissed his wife. 'I'll open the claret when I get back.'

When the lunch was as ready as it could be without the finishing touches, Julia told Catrin to go upstairs and finish drying her hair. 'And don't forget to change your sweater,' she added.

Knowing that the meal she didn't want was eaten at lunchtime purely in her honour, to avoid rushing later when she caught her train, Catrin duly changed her jeans and sweatshirt for narrow grey flannel trousers and the new blue sweater, taking pains with her face and leaving her hair loose, as requested. She decided to go the whole hog, and brushed mascara on her lashes, knowing her mother would applaud the effort she was making. When she was ready she heard a car door slam outside. Good. Richard was back. Then, at the sound of two male voices, her heart skipped a beat. She sighed irritably. Soon, she promised herself, she would stop imagining she could hear

Ashe's voice everywhere, see his dark head in every crowd.

Catrin started down the stairs then stopped dead halfway, her pulse racing. Her imagination had not been playing tricks, after all. Richard *was* back, it was true, but he wasn't alone. Ashe stood in the hall, staring up at her, his face tense. Catrin looked up accusingly as her mother came down to join her, looking her best in the matching blue sweater, her hair swept smoothly into the French twist which suited her face so well.

'I invited him,' said Julia calmly. 'Go on down, please. It's unlucky to pass on the stairs.'

Catrin gave her mother a fulminating look, then went down to face Ashe.

'Hello, Catrin,' he said, his eyes burning in his pale face. 'Your mother invited me to lunch. She said you weren't well.' He looked past her at Julia. 'Good morning, Mrs Harper.'

'Good morning, Ashe. How nice of you to come. Let Richard give you a drink.' She cast a glance at Catrin. 'He took some persuading.'

Catrin stiffened. 'I'm sure he did.'

Ashe took Julia's hand, managing the smile he hadn't been able to summon up for Catrin. 'It's very kind of you to ask me. Under the circumstances.' He turned to Catrin. 'I needed persuading because I knew you wouldn't want me here.'

'So I told him you were ill. Which was only exaggerating a little,' said Julia, unrepentant.

'Well, we're all here together now,' said Richard

with a hint of command as he looked at Catrin. 'So let's have a drink before lunch. I could do with one. I've been on call this weekend,' he added to Ashe, who nodded in understanding.

This time Catrin was not bidden into the kitchen while the men talked medical shop. Julia ordered her to stay and talk to Ashe while the senior members saw to the lunch.

'The one sure way to dry up one's conversation,' said Ashe lightly, when they were alone, 'is to be told to talk to someone. Particularly when it's the last thing you want to do.'

Catrin made no attempt to deny it. 'Look, Ashe, I knew nothing about this,' she assured him.

He nodded coldly. 'If you had you'd have caught the first train back to Pennington.'

'Probably. Though up to now I was enjoying my weekend.'

'I apologise for spoiling it. But Julia was right when she said you weren't well. You look—fragile. Have you seen a doctor?'

Her eyes met his very deliberately. 'I tend to avoid the company of doctors lately.'

'As I know only too well,' he said bitterly. He drank some of the gin and tonic he was holding, and stared into the fire.

He looked older, lines of strain carved into his face, now Catrin could bring herself to look at him properly. He was elegant, as always, in a lightweight tweed suit, but there were marks under his eyes which reminded her of the first time they'd met.

'Did you enjoy your meal at the Chesterton?' he asked abruptly, startling her.

Catrin bit her lip. So he had seen her. 'Yes. I'd never been there before.' The silence which followed this remark brought colour to her face as she remembered the night they should have dined there. And from the look on Ashe's face he was remembering it just as vividly. He drained his glass and set it down so sharply on a table it broke and the glass cut his fingers. He swore involuntarily.

'I'm very sorry. I hope the glass wasn't some priceless heirloom!'

'Never mind the glass,' she said impatiently. 'Let me see your hand.'

'It's nothing much—' He winced as she grabbed it to examine the damage. A pair of small, deep cuts were bleeding profusely.

'Stay there,' she ordered.

She flew upstairs to the medicine chest in the bathroom and took out a bottle of antiseptic and some plasters, grabbed a handful of tissues and ran back down without Julia and Richard being any the wiser.

'I'm afraid some blood dripped on the carpet,' said Ashe.

'Don't worry. I'll get a cloth.' Catrin took his hand and swabbed it with antiseptic, then dried it with tissues and applied two plasters. The moment she'd finished she dropped the slim, strong hand like a hot cake, no more immune to its touch than she'd ever been. 'There. I'll just get something to clear the glass.' She ran off to the kitchen and took a dustpan and brush from the broom cupboard.

'What's up?' said Richard, removing the cork from a bottle of wine.

'Ashe broke a glass and cut himself.'

'Does he need a doctor?' asked Richard with a twinkle in his eye.

'Let Catrin deal with it,' said Julia.

'I have done. I'm afraid he dripped on the carpet a bit.'

'Are you *sure* you don't need me?' demanded Richard.

'No. He'll be fine. I'm not so sure about the carpet.'

'Never mind the carpet!' said Julia impatiently. 'Go and do whatever you have to in a hurry, please, Catrin. Lunch is ready.'

In the sitting room, Ashe was eyeing the damage with some concern. 'I'll pay to have the carpet cleaned, of course.'

'Take my advice, don't offer,' said Catrin curtly, and brushed glass into the dustpan. 'I'll just run the vacuum cleaner over this, then I'll sponge it with clear water. It's only a small stain. No one will notice it among the rose pattern, anyway.'

Ashe watched her downbent head with brooding eyes as she sponged the stain away, but when she got up he was examining his fingers. 'Very neat,' he remarked. 'I couldn't have done better myself.'

'Has she patched you up properly?' said Richard, coming through the doorway. 'My services were turned down.'

*   *   *

Over lunch Catrin found it less effort to be pleasant than she'd expected. Now he was actually here, it was pointless to be hostile to Ashe and ruin the lunch her mother had taken trouble to prepare. And quite apart from that, she admitted to herself, she no longer felt hostile. It was useless to feel angry about the blonde. Ashe was free to do as he liked with his life. It was Catrin who'd sent him away, not the other way round. And just being here with him again was teaching her a salutary lesson. Knowing, now, the agony that jealousy could cause, she was more in sympathy with Ashe on the point than she had been. And, most of all, she wanted him back.

At one point he looked from Catrin to Julia, and smiled a little. 'Last time I was here I didn't think Catrin resembled you at all. Today a stranger could be forgiven for thinking you were sisters.'

'How very flattering, Ashe,' said Julia. 'We have these funny eyes, you see. So if we wear the same colour we match. Otherwise Catrin looks like her father.' She smiled at him and pressed him to more vegetables.

Richard got up to carve more slices from the roast. 'Have some more meat, too,' he said to Ashe. 'Keep your strength up. Because we don't intend to let you get away very early. We need you here this afternoon.'

Catrin looked at him uneasily. 'What for, exactly? Charades, a hand of bridge?'

Julia gave her a quelling look. 'We invited Ashe

here for a purpose. We'll all be better for a good meal beforehand.'

Ashe glanced at Catrin in question, but she shook her head, mystified. 'No use looking at me. I'm not responsible for my parents.'

Richard, smiled at her, pleased, she knew, by her reference to him as a parent.

Ashe smiled at Julia. 'This is the first meal I've enjoyed for some time. The lamb is quite wonderful.'

'Wasn't the food at the Chesterton good last Saturday, then?' said Catrin without thinking and cursed herself as an unholy gleam lit the watchful blue eyes.

'I don't remember what I ate,' he informed her, and smiled at Julia. 'Catrin and I both dined at the Chesterton last week, though not, alas, with each other.'

'Has he said who he was with?' whispered Julia in the kitchen later, as Catrin piled plates into the dishwasher.

'No.'

'But he obviously saw you with Julian.'

'Actually, Julian was very nice to me that night,' said Catrin reprovingly.

'I hope he's nice to you every time he takes you out!'

'I mean, Mother dear, that when I started crying these ''funny'' eyes of mine out on the way home he was very sweet about it, even made coffee for me and let me use his entire box of man-size tissues.'

'Were you crying about Ashe?'

'Of course I was. My first encounter with jealousy reduced me to howling misery.' Catrin pulled a face. 'Which serves me right, I suppose.'

'Why?'

'I got on my high horse and gave Ashe his ring back because of his jealousy and suspicions. Now the boot's on the other foot.' Catrin gave her mother a forlorn look. 'I wasn't jealous because Ashe's lady was so attractive, Mother. I cried because they were talking together nineteen to the dozen, so utterly absorbed in each other I'm amazed Ashe noticed I was there.'

'But he came here today. He didn't really need much persuading, you know.' Julia took her in her arms and kissed her lovingly. 'Come on, darling. Let's take this coffee in and get on with the show.'

'Show?' Catrin eyed her in alarm. 'What do you mean, Mother? You're making me nervous.'

'I'm a bit nervous myself,' admitted Julia. 'But having gone this far I'm determined to go through with it.'

When the four of them were settled round the replenished fire crackling in the stone fireplace, a very edgy Catrin distributed the coffee Julia poured, then resumed her seat to one side of the hearth opposite Ashe. Julia sat very close to Richard on the sofa, as though she needed his support.

'I asked you here today, Ashe, to tell you both a story,' began Julia without preamble. 'I wasn't sure I could rely on Catrin to pass it on to you, Ashe. She's as stubborn as a mule over some things, and I just couldn't see her climbing down off her high horse and getting in touch with you.'

Ashe met Catrin's startled eyes and turned away, realising she was as much in the dark as he.

'It's as plain as the nose on your face,' Richard said bluntly, 'that both of you are pretty miserable with the way things have turned out. Julia was worried that you, Ashe, might not be interested in what we have to say. But in my opinion you wouldn't have come here today if you no longer cared for Catrin.'

The men's eyes met for a moment, then Richard nodded, apparently satisfied. 'You might leave here and never meet any of us again, so it won't matter that you possess more personal knowledge of our family than you might care to.' He smiled affectionately at his stepdaughter. 'With Catrin, of course, it's different. She's stuck with two loving, well-meaning parents whose only aim is to see her happy.'

'I can understand that,' said Ashe quietly, and looked at Catrin, but she was gazing at her mother with troubled eyes. 'I assume,' he added, 'that Catrin has told you I harboured certain—beliefs about her, left over from the first time we met.'

'I gather you thought Liam was your son,' said Julia bluntly, and smiled. 'He really is Richard's son, you know. And I'm his mother, not his granny.'

Ashe smiled fleetingly. 'I've known that for some time, of course. Having met you, it would be difficult to see you as anyone's granny.'

'I had Catrin when I was a month short of my

nineteenth birthday,' said Julia. 'Which is the start of it all.'

Julia Cartwright had gone to work at Tom Hughes's market garden one year during her summer vacation from agricultural college. Tom, a confirmed bachelor in his late forties, had not been welcoming at first, but Julia was good at her job and hard-working. One night there had been a bad storm just as she was about to cycle to her lodgings in the village.

'I was afraid of thunder in those days,' said Julia, 'so Tom took me into the house and cuddled me a bit when the storm was overhead.'

What happened next had been a shock to them both. Tom had suffered agonies of remorse afterwards for what he looked on as the seduction of an innocent young girl.

'That was the trouble,' said Julia dryly. 'If I hadn't been so innocent and Tom hadn't been so unprepared for what happened Catrin wouldn't be here now. When I discovered I was pregnant Tom, a gentleman of the old school, insisted we got married. I was eighteen. Tom was forty-eight.'

Catrin swallowed. 'I never realised—'

'Didn't you sometimes wonder at the age discrepancy?' said Julia gently.

Catrin thought about it. 'Not really. You were just my parents, I suppose. I took it all for granted.' She looked at her mother in appeal. 'But you loved him, didn't you?'

'Of course I did. I never stopped loving him. But

I was never *in* love with him, or he with me. Your father was a lovely man, but almost from the first we were more like father and daughter than husband and wife.'

When Catrin was fifteen Tom Hughes had become ill. He lost weight, found it hard to continue with the work he loved, and was forced to employ a head gardener to take some of the load.

'This is where I come in,' said Richard. 'Tom had bone cancer. I belonged to the medical practice near them, and I was the doctor he came to when he first fell ill. Eventually he was on my visiting list and I came to see him regularly.' He put his arm round Julia. 'This is the difficult part,' he said to Catrin. 'The more I saw of your mother the more I admired her. The way she ran the business and cared for you and Tom at the same time. In short, I fell deeply in love.' He paused to smile down at his wife. 'About that time the chance of the partnership here came up. So, bloody hard as it was to go away, I applied for it. It doesn't do for doctors to fall in love with their patients' wives.'

'When Richard said he was leaving I felt as though my world had ended,' said Julia, and Catrin looked at her, startled.

'Was this before Dad died?'

Julia nodded. 'A couple of months or so. I fell in love too, unknown to Richard. I suffered agonies of guilt, believe me, but no one guessed my secret. Then Tom died, Richard left shortly afterwards, and there we were, Catrin. Just you and me.'

Richard smiled wryly. 'We'd never said a word to each other. Neither of us had a clue how the other felt.'

Catrin relaxed. 'So how did you get together, then?'

'When Richard said goodbye he left his forwarding address,' said Julia, 'so when I wrote the other thank-you letters after the funeral I wrote to him, too, thanking him for his kindness to Tom. Quite apart from my personal feelings for him I was deeply grateful for those evenings when he'd played chess with Tom when I had to work late, and the care he took to make Tom's last days as dignified and free from suffering as he could.'

'You can imagine how I felt when I received her letter,' said Richard. 'So I wrote back. It was the start of a very slow, careful courtship by mail.'

Catrin stared at her mother. 'And of course you were always up first to collect the post. I had no idea.'

'I was afraid to tell you, knowing how you felt about your father,' said Julia, biting her lip. 'I couldn't bear the thought of upsetting you. Then, after months of correspondence, I came up here to stay with Mother,' she said to Ashe. 'Catrin was in France for a week with the school, and I met Richard every day. My mother was all for it. Richard and I spent the entire weekend together before I went home. I saw him very occasionally after that, but only briefly. When Mother broke her wrist it all came to a head, and Richard said we had to bring things out into the open.'

'So why didn't you tell me?' demanded Catrin. 'You knew I liked Richard.'

'Yes. But I wasn't sure how you'd feel about him as a stepfather.' Julia looked at Ashe. 'And you must be wondering why you've been subjected to our family history.'

'I feel privileged,' Ashe assured her, and shot a look at Catrin's face.

Julia smiled at him. 'I told Richard we had to wait until Catrin's exam results were out. I knew she would get into university, but I wanted her to triumph in her own little celebration, when she was all set for college, before I dropped my little bombshell.' She detached herself from Richard's arm and went to a small table between the windows. There were several framed photographs on it, and she returned with one of them and gave it to Ashe.

'Hannah and I had this done for my mother's birthday shortly before you met Catrin.'

Ashe stared at the photograph. Hannah Cartwright and Julia Hughes had their arms round Catrin's shoulders.

'Her three girls, Mother calls it,' said Julia, and turned to Catrin. 'Get up for a minute, darling.'

Catrin got to her feet, eyeing her mother warily. 'Now what?'

'Let's stand together, with our backs to Ashe.'

Catrin obeyed, mystified, then Julia, with a hint of drama, reached up and took the pins from her hair, shaking it loose, then stood beside her daughter, her back to the men.

She turned round, smiling at Ashe, whose eyes were bright with sudden comprehension. 'I was the one in the car, Ashe. Reprehensible for a thirty-seven-year-old woman with a grown-up daughter, I admit. Nevertheless, I was kissing my future husband in a car in broad daylight, only half a mile from my own doorstep. Richard had driven me home from my mother's, and we were finding it very hard to say goodbye. You're about the age now that I was then. Perhaps you can understand how we felt.'

Ashe got to his feet, then very simply, with an apologetic look at Richard, he raised Julia's hand to his lips and kissed it. 'Thank you. I was a jealous fool ten years ago. But I see now why I made such a disastrous mistake. I was utterly certain it was Catrin.'

'The penny didn't drop with me, even when Catrin told me what you thought you'd seen. It was Richard who pinpointed the day, and our session in his car.'

'I remembered how bloody hard it was to part with her,' said Richard with feeling, and got up to peer at the photograph. 'Hannah's a couple of years younger than Julia. The three of them look like sisters in those green dresses.'

'So that's why you insisted we wear the same sweaters today,' said Catrin, eyeing her mother. 'I might have known you had something up your sleeve.'

'It seemed the best way to confess that you were being blamed for my behaviour,' said Julia ruefully. 'And the resemblance is only marked when we wear the same colour.'

Catrin gave her a kiss. 'It never occurred to me it was my mother Ashe saw in the car. I just thought it was some other girl with long brown hair. There's no shortage of them in Wales. What were you wearing?' she added curiously.

'Heavens, darling, I can't remember—'

'A green shirt,' said Ashe, and the others looked at him in surprise. He shrugged. 'I didn't see your face, Julia, but the long, loose hair, just like Catrin's, then Richard's face when he raised it for that particular split second...' He paused. 'I've always remembered every detail of the incident very vividly.'

'So when you met me,' said Richard thoughtfully, 'you assumed Catrin had been playing games with her stepfather.'

Ashe's colour rose slightly, but his eyes were steady. 'I'm afraid so.'

'But you never wore your hair loose, Mother,' said Catrin accusingly. 'And for obvious reasons I remember that day only too well. You had your hair pinned up as usual when you came home.'

Julia blushed like a girl, and Richard grinned lasciviously, putting his arm round her. 'My fault. I'd taken it down—as usual.'

They all laughed together, and suddenly the atmosphere was different.

'It was a great effort to confess all that,' said Julia, looking at her daughter in appeal.

Catrin smiled with loving reassurance. 'I know it was. But you did nothing wrong. You were thirty-seven at the time, Mother, and in spite of all the hard work you did—or maybe because of it—you looked a lot younger than that. And the shirt you were wearing that day was mine—you borrowed it when you went off in such a hurry to see Grandma.'

'Fancy you remembering that!' said Julia, marvelling.

Catrin shot a look at Ashe. 'That day was something I never forgot. Any of it.'

He winced, then looked at Julia and Richard. 'It's a beautiful afternoon. Would you mind if we left you for half an hour and went for a walk?' He turned to Catrin swiftly. 'That is—if you would, Cat. I'd like to talk to you.'

She nodded coolly, more affected by his use of the pet name than she wanted him to know, and Julia smiled in warm approval.

'When you come back I'll have tea ready, and I'll look tidy again.'

'Pity,' said Richard, and grinned at Ashe. 'Go along the footpath to the river. Catrin knows the way.'

Catrin collected her jacket, told her mother they wouldn't be long, then showed Ashe the way through the back garden to a small stile. He vaulted over it and held out his hand to help her over. After a moment's hesitation she took it, but Ashe released it the moment her feet were on the ground on the other side.

They walked along in silence for a while, neither of them eager to break it. The spring sunshine was hazy and surprisingly warm, and in the distance they could hear lambs bleating in counterpoint in the clear air.

'It's a beautiful day,' said Catrin at last, unable to bear the silence any longer.

'Very.'

Again silence, as they walked together along the muddy lane, which was little more than a track leading to the river.

'No one about today,' said Catrin in desperation, her eyes on the sun-dappled water.

'For which I'm grateful,' said Ashe. He stopped to pick up a pebble and tossed it across the water, making it hop three times before it finally sank.

'I've never been able to do that,' she said brightly. 'Liam can.'

'Much as I like Liam, I don't want to talk about him at this moment in time.'

'Which makes a change,' she snapped, and eyed his remote face challengingly. 'What *did* you want to say?'

'Just—I love you,' he said simply, and pulled her into his arms and kissed her in a way which silenced her so effectively she stared at him speechlessly when he raised his head. He smiled into her eyes. 'I thought it best to take you by surprise.'

Catrin drew in a deep, shaky breath, but made no move to pull away. 'It's been quite a day for surprises.'

'Having me turn up as a lunch guest for starters,' he said huskily, then bent and kissed her again, more lingeringly this time, and it took Catrin considerable effort to tear her mouth away.

'The blonde,' she gasped. 'Who *is* she?'

Ashe's arms tightened, his eyes gleaming as they looked deep into hers. 'Were you jealous?'

Her chin lifted haughtily. 'Certainly not.'

'Pity,' he said, and kissed her hard. 'Because I bloody well was, seeing you with that tailor's dummy you're so friendly with.'

Catrin pushed at him in vain. 'Julian was very nice to me that night—' She stopped dead, flushing as Ashe's eyes narrowed.

'Isn't he "nice" to you every night?' he mocked. 'What was so special about that particular night?'

'He'd been given a bonus,' muttered Catrin, looking away, hoping Ashe couldn't feel her heart thumping through her jacket.

'Her name's Helen Radcliffe,' said Ashe abruptly, and moved to lean against a tree, pulling her with him to hold her close in his arms. 'Her husband's the paediatrician at the General, and Helen's a senior registrar, ditto. If you'd left a moment or so later you'd have seen David join us. They were the people who invited me to lunch on another memorable day in our lives. I was repaying their hospitality.'

Catrin couldn't control the sudden relaxation of her body against him, and felt him breathe deeply and hold her closer. 'I was jealous,' she said into his shirtfront.

'Helen's a very attractive woman. But, as you know very well, my taste runs to small brunettes, not statuesque blondes,' Ashe assured her softly.

Catrin raised her head to look at him. 'I wasn't jealous because the lady's a good-looking blonde.'

Ashe's eyes held an expression that made her breathe faster. 'Why, then, darling?'

'Because you were so engrossed in conversation, so interested in each other!'

'Talking shop,' he said wryly, then gave her a triumphant smile. 'But if it made you jealous I'm damn glad we were.' His eyes glittered coldly. 'If it's any consolation, I was jealous as hell at the sight of you with Fellowes.'

Catrin's eyes lit up. 'Were you? I cried my eyes out when he took me home.'

Ashe frowned and gathered her closer. 'Why?'

'Because I was so horribly, sickeningly jealous for the first time in my life. And Julian was very good about it. Made me coffee and mopped me up—'

'And kissed you better?' said Ashe through his teeth.

She shook her head. 'No. I've told you before, he's just a friend.'

'You may be *his* friend, my darling, but I very much doubt he regards you in the same way.' Ashe looked down at her, one eyebrow raised. 'And how did it feel?'

'If you mean the jealousy, it was—unbearable, degrading.' Catrin shuddered.

'Then at last, Catrin, perhaps you can begin to understand how *I* felt, both ten years ago and then again just recently,' he said grimly.

'When you met Richard.'

'Yes.'

They looked at each other for a moment.

'Do you love me?' he asked very quietly.

'Yes.'

'You've had a very odd way of showing it lately.'

Catrin's eyes filled with sudden tears. 'I've been utterly miserable,' she said hoarsely, trying to blink them away, and Ashe bent and kissed her eyes, her nose and her quivering mouth, his lips moving lower to the curve of her throat.

'Can't you tell how much I love you?' she demanded shakily. 'Surely you can feel my heart thumping against you.'

Ashe slid a hand between the lapels of her jacket and laid it flat above her heart, then he kissed her again and she clutched him to her, kissing him back wildly, reaching up to lock her hands round his neck as he caressed her with sudden, fierce need, his heart thudding against her own.

The sound of voices along the footpath brought them back to earth. Ashe chuckled at her desperate attempts to tidy her hair, and smiled warmly at an elderly couple passing by with a panting spaniel.

When the walkers were out of earshot Ashe reached into his breast pocket and brought out the emerald ring. He took her hand, sliding the ring on her finger, and kissed her.

Catrin gave him a wobbly little smile. 'You had this with you, even though you had no idea why Julia had asked you down here?'

Ashe took her hand and began strolling with her, back along the footpath. 'I didn't care a damn why Julia had asked me. All I knew was that you had to be here, and once we were together I had no intention of letting you go again. We've lost enough time through my stupidity. After I saw you last week at the Chesterton I made my mind up we weren't going to lose any more through yours.'

'Oh,' said Catrin, eyes kindling. 'I was stupid, was I?'

Ashe stopped and turned her to face him. 'We've only got one life, Catrin, and it's hellish short. Why spend any of it apart when we could be together?'

Catrin nodded slowly, smiling at him. 'You're right. In this particular instance anyway. But if we do live together—'

'When, not if.'

'Right. *When* we live together don't expect me to agree with you on everything.'

'Of course not,' said Ashe, as they resumed their walk. 'Just on a few major issues, like sharing your life with me, having our children, and so on.'

'I suppose I should be suspicious about the "so on" bit,' said Catrin with a sudden giggle, 'but not today. Let's go and have tea and tell Mother her efforts have not been in vain.'

'She loves you very much,' said Ashe, lifting Catrin over the stile. 'It can't have been easy for her to talk about something so private.'

'No. Mother obviously believes my happiness depends on you.' Catrin eyed him challengingly. 'Can you live with that?'

'Can't live without it. Or you. Let's go and have

tea.' He grinned at her, looking years younger than the man who'd greeted her so warily earlier in the day.

Later that evening, when they were together on Catrin's sofa, talking over the events of the day, Ashe apologised for rushing her away from her family so early.

'I hope your parents understood my pressing need to take you home and hold you in my arms like this.'

'It can't have escaped your notice,' said Catrin dryly, 'that, although Richard's been married to my mother for ten years or so, he feels exactly the same about *her*. They understood, believe me.'

'I'm glad. Tell me you love me again.'

'I don't love you *again*. I love you still,' she corrected, and kissing him with an emphasis meant to underline her words. 'I hope Mother didn't embarrass you with her talk of weddings.'

'Not in the least.' Ashe stretched luxuriously, and pulled her onto his lap. 'But, having succeeded in getting the ring back on your finger, I was content to tread softly. You don't like being pushed, remember.'

'True,' said Catrin, wondering how to let him know she didn't mind being pushed on that particular subject any more. A trial period of living together was totally unnecessary. The experiences of the past few weeks had taught her that life without Ashe was meaningless. A lesson she'd learned the hard way.

Catrin slid to her feet and stood looking down at him, her hands behind her back. 'Actually...' she be-

gan, then cleared her throat nervously. 'What I'm trying to say—' She sighed, eyeing Ashe mutinously as
he showed no signs of helping her out. 'The thing is,
Ashe, if we intend having children, I suppose it would
be tidier all round if we got married first,' she finished
in a rush.

Ashe rose to his feet slowly, and stood looking
down at her. 'Was that a proposal, by any chance,
Cat? If so, it was barely recognisable. Are you saying
you're marrying me just to make things easier for
these children we haven't had yet?'

'No,' she muttered, flushing, then looked at him
through her lashes. 'I could show you why,' she offered.

Ashe took his jacket off, his eyes never leaving
hers. 'Ah, but are you likely to convince me?'

'I can try,' she said demurely, and turned suddenly
and raced towards the bedroom, but Ashe caught her,
laughing, and picked her up.

'I'm carrying you across the threshold,' he said,
kissing her nose.

'Isn't that supposed to happen some other time?'
she said, breathless.

'Tonight,' he said, suddenly serious, 'it seems very
appropriate.'

Hours later, they were still awake in each other's
arms, loath to waste any time in sleep. After the first,
fierce joy of reconciliation was over they talked long
into the night, bridging the gap of their separation,
acknowledging how close they'd come to wrecking
each other's lives.

'I can't imagine, now, why I gave you back the ring,' said Catrin. 'Sheer melodrama. I was sorry the moment I'd done it.'

'So was I,' he said sombrely. 'When you posted it back it was like a kick in the teeth.'

'I'm sorry.'

'Show me.'

'Willingly.'

The process of consolation was so satisfactory that it was some time before Ashe spoke again.

'I suppose I'm an anachronism in this day and age.'

'In what way?'

'I'm marrying my first love.'

Catrin reached out to switch on her bedside lamp, then propped herself up on one elbow to look down into his face. 'Ashe, you were twenty-eight when I first met you. Surely you must have been in love before?'

'Of course. Several times.' Ashe looked up into her eyes. 'But I'd never really loved anyone until I met you. I knew you for only two short weeks, yet after that nothing was ever the same for me again until I saw a battered little face on a pillow in Pennington General.'

Catrin went down into his upstretched arms, her cheek against his. 'And yet we came so close to losing our second chance.' She shivered, and he held her tightly.

'Don't. I won't let you go again, no matter how many times you throw my ring back at me,' Ashe assured her.

'I won't again.' She smiled up at him. 'Just in case you keep it.'

'Good thinking!'

There was silence while both of them gloried in the peace and joy of being in each other's arms.

'It's the same for me, Ashe,' said Catrin, after a time.

'What, exactly? Are you pinching yourself, too, just to make sure you aren't dreaming?' he said, kissing her.

'That too,' she agreed happily. 'But I meant the first love bit. You're mine, too, as you very well know.' She gave him a glittering, incandescent smile. 'First love, last love, or—to quote someone very near and dear to me—the love of my life.'

Modern Romance™
...seduction and
passion guaranteed

Tender Romance™
...love affairs that
last a lifetime

Medical Romance™
...medical drama
on the pulse

Historical Romance™
...rich, vivid and
passionate

Sensual Romance™
...sassy, sexy and
seductive

Blaze Romance™
...the temperature's
rising

27 new titles every month.

Live the emotion

MILLS & BOON®

PENNINGTON

Catherine George
PENNINGTON
Bargaining with the Boss

BOOK TEN

Available from 2nd April 2004

MILLS & BOON

PASSIONATE
PROTECTORS

Lori Foster
Donna Kauffman
Jill Shalvis

Three brand-new novellas
– packed full of danger and desire!

On sale 2nd April 2004

Available at most branches of WHSmith, Tesco, Martins, Borders,
Eason, Sainsbury's and all good paperback bookshops.

A Mother's Day Gift

A collection of brand-new romances just for you!

Margaret Way
Anne Ashley
Lucy Monroe

On sale 5th March 2004

*Available at most branches of WHSmith, Tesco, Martins, Borders,
Eason, Sainsbury's and all good paperback bookshops.*